THE MERCURIAL SCIENCE OF THE HUMAN HEART

THE
MERCURIAL SCIENCE
OF THE
HUMAN HEART

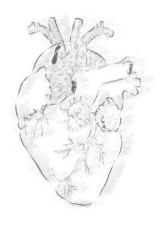

Vincent Reusch

New Rivers Press

50th Anniversary
1968-2018

©2018 by Vincent Reusch
First Edition
Library of Congress Control Number: 2018930072
ISBN: 978-0-89823-370-4
eISBN: 978-0-89823-371-1

New Rivers Press is a nonprofit literary press associated with
Minnesota State University Moorhead.

Cover and interior design by Brittany Schultz and Trista Conzemius
Author photo by Heather A. Slomski

The publication of *The Mercurial Science of the Human Heart* is made
possible by the generous support of Minnesota State University
Moorhead, the Dawson Family Endowment, and other contributors
to New Rivers Press.

NRP Staff: Nayt Rundquist, Managing Editor; Kevin Carollo, Editor;
Travis Dolence, Director
Thomas Anstadt, Co-Art Director; Trista Conzemius, Co-Art Director

Interns: Trevor Fellows, Laura Grimm, Kendra Johnson,
Anna Landsverk, Mikaila Norman, Lauren Phillips, Ashley Thorpe,
Cameron Schulz, Rachael Wing

The Mercurial Science of the Human Heart **book team:** Trevor Fellows,
Aubrey Johnson, Anna Landsverk, Dayton Lien

 Printed in the USA on acid-free, archival-grade paper.

The Mercurial Science of the Human Heart is distributed nationally by
Small Press Distribution.

New Rivers Press
c/o MSUM
1104 7th Ave S.
Moorhead, MN 56563
www.newriverspress.com

CONTENTS

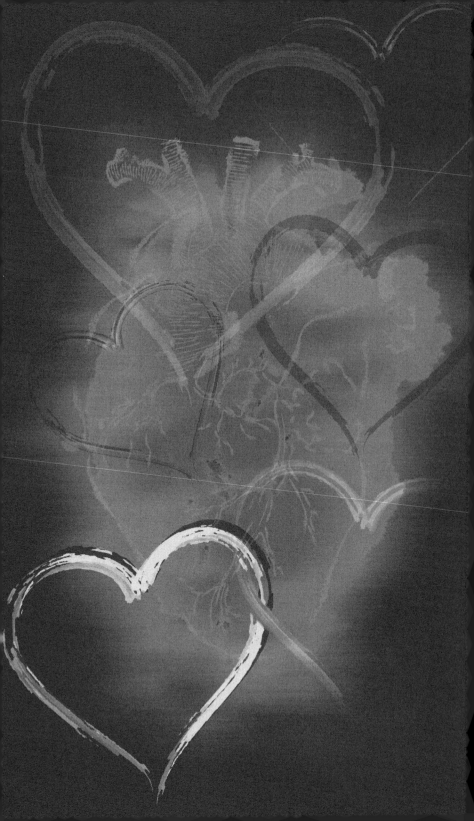

THE MERCURIAL SCIENCE OF THE HUMAN HEART

No one notices the tumult of Norah's walk to work—the somersaults, the aerial walkovers, the faceplants, her body peeling from the sidewalk, a paper-doll curl that sets her upright and wobbling just in time to return the wave from Billy, the line cook at The Flatiron, and again in time to insert her key into the front door of VanBochove's Flowers. Ever since she left Steve, took Adeline and moved into her new apartment, the world for Norah has refused to stand still.

Before work this morning, she moved from sink to stove by way of the space of wall above her kitchen table. On her way to the toaster, she used the ceiling light as a sling, grabbing hold as she floated by, whirling like Apollo 13 around the dark side of the moon, like a breadcrumb that won't quite wash down the drain. She's learned to roll with these motions of her apartment, these motions of the world—for though she knows that from the perspective of others she is the one unhinged, to her it is the world untethered, the planet a cosmic gutter ball, banging through the trough on its way to the dark mystery at the end of the lane. She managed to keep Addy's plate of scrambled eggs and toast upright until she could deposit it on the table along with a

"You're welcome," to which her daughter, between her headphones, made no reply.

Only inside the flower shop do the world's motions calm, and then Norah suffers only an occasional tremor as a customer speaks of a wedding anniversary, or of a wife, or a girlfriend, or any woman whose name happens to be two syllables and ends in *y* (or *ie*—or once just *i*, as in Candi). But most of her business between holidays is for hospital rooms and funeral parlors, and in these contexts when an order comes for the bedside or the memorial of a Mandy or a Marcie or a Candi she's able to smooth her shirt, perhaps to smile, and to create an arrangement so lavish that it borders on celebratory.

This morning, Norah's work is sober as she prepares a funeral arrangement for Mrs. Potsdam, who had been her twelfth-grade science teacher. Norah has never forgotten the lecture Mrs. Potsdam gave on the concept of a block universe, how she had said that there is no flow of time in a block universe, no motion at all, but instead a model of the entirety of time and space, complete in every detail. Think of a cartoon flip book, Mrs. Potsdam had said, the book being the whole of reality and each panel a snapshot of a moment in time. You feel as if your life is unfolding, but, in fact, the book is already written. This theory had lodged itself somewhere near the surface of Norah's consciousness, so that even now she remembers it often and with great sadness—each version of herself as whole as the next, each filled with a full measure of hope, a full measure of love, of grief, each trapped on her own page unable to touch the others.

Norah weaves angel-choir lilies and black dahlias into Mrs. Potsdam's wreath, filling the gaps with heather and smooth aster. When the arrangement is finished she cleans the workbench. She culls the flowers in the cooler, clips stems, and transfers bouquets to buckets of fresh water. This is her favorite part of the day, the greenhouse aroma of wet stems more moving to her, somehow more essential, than the dry perfumes of the blooms. And for a time, gravity operates on Norah in the same predictable manner that led Einstein to his general theory of relativity.

When lunchtime arrives, she flips the 'open' sign that hangs in the window to the 'back at' sign, with its hands that point always to one o'clock. For a moment, she stands inside the open front door, arms hanging heavily at her sides until the blood tingles in her fingertips. Then she takes one trepidatious step, and then another. And then, just as she begins to smile, the world tilts, and Norah spills onto the sidewalk.

She lunches every day now at The Flatiron, not because she likes the food, but because the walk is only half a block and not so painful as the walk to The Terrace, where she used to meet Steve for lunch. She sits in her usual place, the corner booth with the view out the window. From here she can see The Clothes Post, Meyer Hardware, and, on the far side of the alley, Crossroads Bank where Steve works in investments.

Billy takes her order of egg salad and soup of the day—tomato bisque. Billy is always there to take her order, stepping from behind the counter, past the waitress.

Billy graduated from high school last year, and though he talks about college Norah doesn't believe he'll go. She doesn't think he lacks ambition, but there is a languor about him that makes her think he's in no hurry. It is a languor that shows in the time it takes him to cross the room, in the long, slow motion of his arm as he places an order on the counter, and in his smile, which is slow to dawn, not sinister but lightheartedly conspiratorial, as if in response to some subtext playing out between him and his co-conspirator. He is strong and long-limbed, was the quarterback of his high school football team, and Norah sometimes imagines him in a game, standing in the pocket while the defense converges, looking downfield as if he has all the time in the world.

Norah and Steve had dinner at Billy's parents' house years ago, and she remembers Billy watching them as they sat in the dining room drinking wine. An hour after his parents had put him to bed, they discovered Billy eavesdropping from behind the couch. He was wearing only his underwear, and the image of him in his white briefs sticks with Norah. He was eleven or twelve years old and was in the middle of a growth spurt, so that his legs and hips seemed those of a man, his upper body still a boy's.

As Billy writes her order on his pad, his pencil moving evenly and unhurried from letter to letter, Norah adds, "And a sparkling water." She sits with her knees braced against the bottom of the table, the diner rocking as if she is in the galley of a ship at sea.

"Soda water off the gun okay?" he asks.

"Sure," she says.

Norah is looking out the window when Billy returns with her food. He runs a dishtowel over her table and flips it onto his shoulder before he sets down her plate, bowl, and glass.

When Norah says, "Thank you," Billy smiles as if her thank you means something more. He slips his hand into his front pants pocket. His t-shirt is short and untucked, and as his hand presses into the pocket his pants slide down to expose the waistband of his underwear—not white briefs now but blue-striped boxers, above them a strip of tanned flesh, a thin line of dark hair bisecting his stomach.

"Say hello to your mother for me," Norah says.

Billy nods once, cracks a smile like a wink and says, "I'll do that." When he's gone, Norah turns back to the window and sees, through the steam of her tomato bisque, Steve walking down the alley, and buffeting in his wake, as a scrap of burned paper rises on the convection of air above a fire, a black and charred thing the height of a woman.

Adeline stands in the lunch line. She looks at a cheeseburger, its cheese melted just right, and feels a pull deep inside herself, a hunger as acute as thirst, but she moves on to the cottage cheese and pineapple plate. Because, well, fuck them. She waits for the server to hand her a plate, but after the woman serves the girl in front of her, she serves two boys, football players who ask for two burgers each. Adeline waits as the boys walk past. But the server moves on to the next student in line, and the next, and, okay, fuck you too.

She carries her tray to the salad bar, places on it four baby carrots, six celery sticks, and a hardboiled egg. She sits at a table with two girls with whom she had been close friends last year, but who both showed up at school this year ensconced in relationships. Their boyfriends are sitting across from them, and Adeline sits on the girls' side, one seat removed. She asks for the salt, but one of the boys speaks at the same moment and no one hears her. The boy is saying something about a campfire and vodka, an inside joke, and the four break into laughter. No one looks at Adeline, though she feels, as she pretends she is part of the laughter, as if everyone in the lunchroom is looking at her. She nods tiny imperceptible nods as the others at the table nod, laughs tiny imperceptible laughs as they laugh. When she peels her hardboiled egg, one of the boys sniffs the air and rises from his seat, a mockery of a man on a mission, and says to the room, "All right, folks. Who's ripping the juicy ones?"

Steve drops his keys onto a small table inside the front door of his house. He slips off his shoes and walks to the kitchen, enveloped in a fog of thought that clings to him, warm and moist. He pulls a glass from a tall cupboard, turns it upright on the counter and pours in bourbon from a crystal decanter. As he fills the glass halfway and then a splash more, he sees that the dining-room table is gone. He tries to remember if it was there this morning. He thinks it was. Or maybe it wasn't. Maybe it has been gone for days. He leaves the stopper off the decanter, walks to the living room, and sits in a recliner chair in front of his television. Beside his chair is a TV tray, the only other furniture in the living room, on it a lamp and remote control. He sets down his drink, picks up the remote, and turns on the TV. The local news appears, the commentators young, the anchor's suit a size too big.

Steve looks again at the space of dining room where the table had been. The chairs are still there—upright, throne-like, six of them standing formally in two straight lines. He tries once more to remember if the table had been there this morning, but his act of remembrance is insincere, a ploy designed to keep his mind away from those primordial thoughts that fill his house with such humidity and rank, swamp air.

But the ploy doesn't work—the gaseous pool of unexamined thought and the static of anxiety too volatile a combination to suppress—and the thoughts spark to life, single-celled, born in the roots of his sympathetic and parasympathetic nervous systems. A flash and there are Norah's eyes following his phone as he slips it still ringing into his pocket. A flash and there is Adeline, framed in his car's rearview mirror, standing in her socks in the driveway. A flash and Brandy's thighs press against his ears, the sharp insistence of her fingers on the back of his head.

Born, the thoughts grow, wet and embryonic. Amoebae emerge from the pores of his skin, flagella whipping, cilia gyrating. Larval mosquitos slide down his temples. Newly hatched snails, shell-less, ride their slicks of mucous down his neck. The thoughts dampen his starched, white shirt. They moisten the bottoms of his socks, cause black-mold footprints to form, invisible, on the underside of the oak floor. The organisms evolve, molt, and fly into the air, thickest in the space between his easy chair and the television, so that when he goes to bed he often realizes that he has seen nothing of what was on the screen.

Now, as he sits in the growing dusk he feels the first hatching of larvae against his skin, hears the soft tear of cocoons, and the insects rise. His phone rings, and he pulls it from his pants pocket. It is Adeline. He answers, but he has a hard time hearing, her voice distant, hollow, as if she is standing at the far end of a long tunnel. And on his end she is drowned out by something large and winged—a dragonfly?—that circles his head. She asks if they're still on for Sunday. "Sure," he says. He thinks, "Sunday, Sunday, Sunday," and the word swirls around him, an echo that vibrates through a chorus of insect wings. He hears Adeline say, "The Flatiron," and he says, "Yes, breakfast." Something large bumps his ear, and he drops the phone and swats at the air around his head. When he puts the phone back to his ear, Adeline is not there.

He looks for a while toward the television, blinking as the insects brush his eyelashes. Then he taps Brandy's name on his phone and raises it to his ear. "It's me," he says. A cloud of tiny moths swarms in the phone's blue light. "No," he says. "I just wanted to talk. I just feel—" A boy on the news says, "Hot tomorrow. Humidity near one hundred percent," and Steve says, "I feel like I just want to talk." He says, "No. Of course not," and he says, "Yes, of course." A tadpole slides from his nostril, and he sniffs it back up and says, "Okay. The door's open. Let yourself in."

At twenty after nine Adeline sits in a window booth at The Flatiron, the booth she's always shared with her father during their Sunday breakfasts, a routine that dates back further than her memory. She won't say that she's missed these breakfasts, and so she won't say that she blames her mother for their ending.

She's drinking coffee—she wants to be a coffee drinker—and she looks often up the street as she takes small sips from her mug. At nine-thirty she pulls her phone from her purse and calls her father. When he doesn't answer she leaves a message. "I'm here," she says. "I've been here for half an hour."

She waits another fifteen minutes before she walks to the counter to pay for her coffee. No one is at the register, and no one answers when she leans over the counter and says, "Hello?" She calls again, and when no one comes, she puts down a five-dollar bill.

As she's walking away from The Flatiron, Adeline sees her father's car driving toward her. He's speeding. She steps forward, but he doesn't slow. And as he races past she sees, through a film of steam on his windows, the silhouette of a woman in the passenger seat. The woman is thin and dark and perfectly rigid. Then the car is gone, racing up the hill, a trail of black exhaust in its wake.

Norah lies on her back in bed, an empty Burgundy glass and an open issue of Vogue on her nightstand. Her arms lie at her sides, immobile as iron posts, her fight with gravity finished for the day.

Her eyes are open, her head turned toward the window where Steve sits in his car, driving. He is both here, floating in the darkness outside her window, and somewhere else. Norah doesn't know how this can be, but she suspects that it has to do with affinity, some bond between them strong enough to warp space, open a wormhole, a quantum door, and to connect these two bodies in sympathetic union. A penumbra of dissonance encircles his car, where the darkness of his night transitions to the darkness of her own. The road treadmills under the car's wheels. Steve squints against a flash of headlights and yells, "Brights, dickhead!"

His phone rings, and he pulls it from his jacket pocket, looks at it, and puts it down on the passenger seat. From the hallway outside her bedroom door, Norah hears Addy say, "Where were you? Why don't you ever, ever answer your phone? This isn't fair. I hate it here." Then Norah hears the tinny whisper of Addy's headphones, which fades with the closing of the bathroom door.

Steve spins the steering wheel. The car slows and rocks to a halt. His windows are down, and the sound of crickets rises as he cuts the engine. He pulls a pewter flask from his armrest, opens it, drinks, and screws the cap back on. A minute passes, and he puts away the flask and picks up his phone. He touches the screen, and his face glows blue. When the light dims, he touches the screen again. Then he taps the phone twice, quickly, raises it to his ear, and Norah's phone rings from the top of her dresser.

Norah tries to rise, but she can't. Breathing is hard enough, the weight of the world pressing her down. She relaxes, and then heaves, as if to surprise something— the world? herself? she's not sure. A lock of hair slides down her forehead and tickles her ear. The phone turns circles as it rings.

Then the ringing stops, and the hinges of a screen door creak somewhere in the darkness outside Steve's car. A woman says in a dry, coarse whisper, "What are you doing? Get in here before someone sees you." Steve puts his phone back into his pocket, and as he opens his car door an overpowering, bitter scent drifts into Norah's bedroom, the scent of a home gutted by fire.

―――――――――― ―――――――――――

Adeline sits in the back corner of the classroom, her hand raised. Ms. Halverson has just asked the class what makes Frankenstein's monster a round character.

Adeline plans to say that it's because Victor gave him a human heart and then broke it, and that anyone with a broken heart is a complex character. All the creature wants, Adeline will tell the class, is to be seen, to be really seen. But Victor doesn't see him. No one sees him. He's an eight-foot-tall monster, but he's also invisible. And that breaks the creature's heart. And when someone's heart is broken, really broken, that person is capable of anything.

Adeline won't tell the class that the book made her cry.

It wasn't while she was reading that she cried, but afterward, as she lay in bed and thought how confused the creature must have been. How frightened. How hopeful that Victor would come back and put his arms around him, tell him that it's okay, that everything is going to be okay. She won't tell Ms. Halverson how she imagines putting her own arms around the creature. How she imagines the two of them living alone together in a cabin in the woods. How they will eat fresh game that he will catch, and how in the evenings they will sit in front of the fire and drink tea and read together. How the bed will be covered in wolf skins, and how the room will smell like cedar.

She wants to believe that anyone who reads the book will feel for the creature. That they'll recognize themselves in him. But as she waits with her hand in the air and hears the comments of other students—"I didn't really get it," and, "I'd of blown his head off," and, "I think he might have been gay"—she realizes that she's wrong. These aren't people who are interested in understanding. They're the stone-throwing townsfolk, the torch-wielding mob from the Boris Karloff film.

The room is quiet now. Ms. Halverson looks over the class, eyebrows raised in a theatrical gesture of anticipation. "Well?" she says, and Adeline raises her hand higher, embarrassed by her need to share, resentful of Ms. Halverson for making her show it.

"Anyone?" says Ms. Halverson.

Then the bell rings. Adeline puts down her hand, and the students pack up their books and shuffle from the room like monsters.

Norah is once again lying on her back in bed, the full force of gravity pressing her down, her cellphone cradled in her immobile hand. Steve sits again outside her window. He's not in his car tonight but sitting in the darkness in his recliner chair, his face pale in the glow of his cellphone.

Steve bounces his phone against his knee, wipes his forehead with a scrap of paper towel. Wipes it again. Then he presses a button and raises the phone to his ear.

Norah works her ossified thumb over to the answer key. A second passes, and then two, and then she hears Steve's voice outside her window. "It's me. Can you get away?" There is a pause, and then he says, "Okay. Let yourself in. I'll be in the shower."

The wormhole follows Steve into his bedroom, and as he strips and steps into the shower, the weight of gravity doubles, quadruples, and Norah turns away.

When she smells smoke, Norah looks again, sees a curl of ash blow through his bedroom door. Steve steps from the shower, and the ash pulls itself into the shape of a woman. "Look at you," the woman says in the tone-less voice of a lifelong smoker. Steve crosses the floor to her, and she wraps him in a vaporous embrace and lowers him onto the bed.

Norah closes her eyes, but she hears them. She always hears them—the dry cracking moan of the woman, Steve's thick wet breath. When she looks again—she always looks again; how can she help it, and who can blame her?—she sees the pulsing moon of his bare butt, and, sliding over his pale flesh, the long slender fingers of a thin, charred hand.

Steve's mattress is damp and sticky, the air around him thick with his thoughts. Thick with one thought, especially, that had been a larva in his tear duct when he'd awoken. As he lay in the darkness, the thought had grown into a grub, crawled down his cheek, affixed itself, and transformed into a pupa. Now it emerges—long and twiggy, with two thin, straight wings—and flies around his head. Every so often it passes close enough to his ear that he can hear embedded in the buzz of its wings his own voice, just a word or two—"wouldn't have," and "my needs," and "more attention"—fragments of the single sentence that the insect's wings beat out again and again, the words piecing themselves together in random orders to create poetic variations of "Maybe if you would have paid a little more attention to my needs, this wouldn't have happened."

The toilet flushes. He looks at the alarm clock beside his bed. Three-twenty-two a.m. Water runs in the sink, and then the bathroom door opens and Brandy steps out. She's rubbing lotion into her hands and along her forearms. She reaches down and rubs along her inner thighs, but, even so, when she climbs on top of Steve they scrape, hard and dry, against his hips. She reaches for a tube of ChapStick that stands on end on the nightstand, and as her breasts pass above Steve's face, the twiggy insect's wings curl up and it falls, a dry husk, onto the pillow beside his ear.

Steve puts his mouth around Brandy's breast. It is at first dry and brittle and tasting of ash, but it softens as it pulls the mucous from his tongue. He puts his mouth around her other breast as she uncaps the ChapStick, and as his mouth grows drier around her softening nipple, he hears the sizzle of ChapStick against her lips. He pulls her down to him, rubs her breasts on his face until the swamp air around him dries and he has no thoughts except those of her breasts, and of her thighs that rock now, ever more supple, against his groin.

An hour passes, and when they've finished, her hip is soft and damp beneath his hand, his skin cool and dry and no longer smelling of mushrooms. They lie still for half an hour, he without thought, she without need. Then he feels a tickle of mucus sliding somewhere along the contour of his inner ear, and she reaches to the nightstand for a pump of lotion.

Adeline sits inside her closet rereading *Frankenstein*. She is nested in a pile of dirty clothes, a reading lamp clipped to the metal bar above her head, her phone on the floor beside her. It is past three a.m. She has been in the closet since early evening when she moved from her bed to avoid her mother, who walked by so often, tripping every time she passed Adeline's bedroom door. When the door was open, her mother would turn her face up from the floor and smile her crooked, broken smile that pretended to say, "Oops, did it again," but that really said, "Please save me." And when Adeline closed the door it was no better, the thump and the silence, the shuffle of shadow in the crack at the door's bottom.

Adeline began her rereading of *Frankenstein* from chapter eleven, when the "wretch" takes over to tell his tale of unnatural birth, wandering, and banishment. She has no interest in Victor's narration. She does not pity him. Does not forgive. Today, she is at the scene where the creature lingers after killing the boy, lingers and thinks of Victor, the wretch's somehow father. "'For some days I haunted the spot where these scenes had taken place,'" she reads, "'sometimes wishing to see you, sometimes resolved to quit the world and its miseries forever.'"

She touches her phone, and the screen brightens and fades. It has been a week since her father didn't stop outside The Flatiron. He has not called. No one has called. For weeks. No texts. No emails. No hellos in the hallway at school. No replies to her Facebook posts. No questions from teachers about missing work or absences from class.

She turns back to her book and reads until her legs are numb, until Victor, in his desolate cottage laboratory, tears to pieces the creature's half-constructed bride-to-be, and the creature stands among the torn flesh and swears revenge, "'revenge, henceforth dearer than light or food!'" She lingers over these words. She imagines herself speaking them, but when she tries, she is self-conscious, her voice tremulous. She reads on until she comes to the end of the novel, and when she closes the book she runs through her mind another of the creature's lines. When she speaks this one it feels right: "'But soon I shall die, and what I now feel be no longer felt.'"

As Norah carries the Hungry Man TV dinners to the table, she almost collapses under their weight, their density increasing by a level of magnitude each time she thinks to herself—Salisbury steak; I'm serving Salisbury steak—these two TV dinners at the center of the black hole of her life. Every mistake she's ever made, every missed opportunity, every wrong turn, compressed into these two dense pieces of meat. Salisbury steaks the weight of cargo ships. Of a thousand cargo ships.

Norah's pulse beats painfully in the side of her face. She had a mishap earlier today at the Flatiron. Billy was at the counter wrapping silverware in paper napkins, and, when he nodded to greet her, gravity let go of Norah—just for one beat, just long enough for her feet to float into the air behind her, before it reignited and she dropped, a cosmic joke, upsy daisy, the rug pulled out from beneath her. Her head came down on a table, a clatter as everything jumped—the bowl of creamers, the plate of butter pads, the salt and pepper shakers. Billy looked down at the paper strip he had been winding around his napkin, and when he glanced back up, gravity wavered again, and again Norah was lifted and dropped, quick and violent, and, yes, it hurt. She was able to turn her face to the side before the collisions, the same side both times, and now as she calls Adeline to the dinner table, that side of her jaw feels like someone else's. She wishes it were someone else's.

After several minutes Adeline appears in the dining room. She's dressed in black, a black sheer sarong wrapped around a black miniskirt over fishnet stockings. Everything is a size too small, and Norah wishes she didn't notice, wishes she didn't care. Adeline pulls her headphones down to her neck and looks at the six tall chairs around the table, ridiculous in the small apartment. She slides into the one farthest from her mother and pulls her TV dinner toward herself. "Are you expecting four other people?" she asks. "Where's Dad eating? On his floor?"

Norah grips the edge of the table as the room sways. "Frankly," she says, "I don't give a damn."

"I bet you don't," Adeline says. She pokes at her mashed potatoes. They are dry along the edges, and as she runs her fork over them they peel up, retaining the shape of the tray's compartment. She pokes at her vegetable medley and apple cobbler. Then she takes a small bite of the potatoes, another of the meat. When she sees that Norah is watching, she says, "Jesus. What?"

They eat in silence until Adeline puts down her fork, sighs, and says, "Okay, how was work?"

Norah has just taken a bite of Salisbury steak. It's too hot, and she tries to blow on it while it is in her mouth. She holds up her finger, and Adeline shakes her head and looks away.

"It was okay," Norah finally says. "I did an arrangement for a girl's baptism."

"Maybe I should be re-baptized."

"Why do you say that?"

"I think I'm invisible."

"I see you."

"You don't count."

A spasm passes through Norah's wounded face, and Adeline says, "I didn't mean that. I think I have Tourette's or something. Can I go now?"

After Norah finishes her dinner, she throws away the trays, washes the silverware, and sits in the living room holding an ice pack against her face. She turns on the TV. An infomercial. Save the Children. As the bearded host walks with a little girl down a garbage-strewn street, Norah thinks how unfair that second hit was at The Flatiron—how maddeningly, comically unfair.

She had spent her afternoon telling herself that the second blow hadn't been as painful as the first, hadn't been as shocking. She told herself that one gets used to a thing. That people adapt. That though the second hit was regrettable, it was, in a way, part of the first. That both were, in a way, part of this one event in her life. She thought of frequency and multiplicity, the principle of diminishing returns. But now, as her fingers grow cold against the ice, and the bearded man on TV (Meathead, she thinks—then she remembers: Rob Reiner) tells her that twenty-one thousand children die each day of malnutrition and preventable diseases, she sees with complete clarity that there is no such thing in nature as a principle of diminishing returns, that twenty-one thousand children dying of malnutrition is twenty-one-thousand times the tragedy of a single dying child. And that one million suffering is one million times the tragedy of one. This fact is difficult to digest. It's like trying to understand the size of a galaxy, or the rate of expansion in the first nanosecond of the Big Bang. There are times—most of the time, most of her life—when Norah's mind can't encompass it. But she realizes now that, for an instant, each time her body swings into a table, a wall, a ceiling, the fact is as real and solid as the fact of her own pain. And in these nanoseconds of grace, she feels the tens of millions of people who are hurting. There they are in her flash of pain, stars in a moonless desert sky.

Before the infomercial ends, Norah finds her cellphone, a pen, and pad of paper, and she calls the number on the screen. The woman on the other end of the line tells her what her dollar-a-day will provide for her sponsored child, and when Norah commits, the woman tells her the child's name—Alejandro.

As Norah writes the name on her pad of paper, she hears Adeline behind her. Just her breath, a quick disgusted sound, and then her voice, "Oh yay, I finally get a little brother." When Norah turns around, the hallway is empty. Even so, she hears the tinny whisper of Adeline's headphones, and she shouts toward Adeline's bedroom door, "Those better not be on your ears that loud!"

Steve drops his keys onto the round table by the door, realizing only when they hit the floor that the table is gone. Last week, the dining chairs disappeared. Next week he supposes his La-Z-Boy will go. He doesn't care, and though his lack of concern unnerves him, he can't help but think that there is something right in this, his shrinking world.

He pours a bourbon, sits in his La-Z-Boy, and finds that the lamp is missing from the TV tray. Then he sees that the TV is missing. He pulls his phone from his pocket and sees two missed calls from Addy. He switches on the ringer and sets the phone on the table beside his bourbon. It is evening, and the room is lit with twilight, the half hour of the day when he most suffers. The air thickens around him, and the warm sludge of his thought coats his skin.

He thinks of his first kiss with Brandy as they stood beside the dumpster in the alley behind the bank. It was clumsy, her mouth open too wide, the flick of her tongue sudden and shocking. All of it so wrong. The wrong lips, the wrong tongue. It was the day after this kiss, while he was shaving, that the first tiny slug appeared. He thought at first that he'd cut himself, a ribbon of red rinsing out of his razor. But then he saw against the white porcelain of the sink the gray soft half-body, and on his cheek the other half, and the bright red disk of its bisection.

He thinks of how he clung to Norah for a week after that. He rented a cottage on the lake and took the family there for the weekend. He pulled Norah and Addy on waterskis behind the boat, and they all ate hotdogs around the fire. He thinks now of how Addy said "gross" when he pulled Norah into his lap and kissed her as the coals glowed in the fire pit. And how Addy smiled after she said that, and he could see that she was thinking about whatever boy had been inhabiting her daydreams of late.

Then there was the second time with Brandy, after a week of her anxious glances, her jaw-pulsing and fingernail biting. This time she met him in the employee bathroom, coming in as he opened the door to go out. This time with her hand on his groin, her fingers wrapping him, claw-like, and he had known—he admits now, as the pupae molt and the insects rise from his body—he had known that her grip was both real and metaphor. To extricate himself would be nearly impossible. The affair would run its course, would come out, would shatter his marriage. He couldn't say why he took the first step down that path, only that he felt pulled, perhaps that Brandy's need was stronger than his ability to resist.

The twilight deepens to darkness as Steve thinks and the insects multiply and swirl, the buzz of their wings beginning to coalesce, to synchronize, to become speech, Norah's voice tonight. There is the "Hello? This is she," when Norah answered the phone on that evening, the words high and fast and insectoid, encircling him, repeating. Hello? This is she. Hello? Hello? This is she, is she, is she. Hello? Then there is only the susurration of wings, the silence as Norah held the phone to her ear while Steve looked on from his seat beside her on the couch, realizing by the twitching of her face who was on the other end of the line. There is only this soft buzz of wings, the static on the line, the sawing of the string section in the orchestra pit, faster and faster, and then the crescendo, Norah's sharp wail, reproduced in miniature through the wings of the thousand leggy insects that fill the darkness around Steve.

A backpack lies on Adeline's bed. It is long and covered with webbing and straps, a pack meant for camping or for Eurail tours, the pack she used for basketball camp the summer before she quit the team. A sleeping bag is lashed to its bottom.

She told her mother that she's going to her father's house for the weekend. And this is true, though it won't just be for the weekend. She hasn't told her father that she's coming, that she plans to stay. She will not say it in a voicemail. And besides, she is his daughter. She has a right. She slides *Frankenstein* into an outside pocket and hoists the bag onto her shoulders.

"I wish you wouldn't," Adeline's mother says as Adeline steps into the hallway.

The hallway has become her mother's haunt, the hemmed-in ground where she can block the way, force conversation.

"His house isn't a healthy place to be," her mother says.

"And your house is," Adeline says. She tries to step by; her mother moves into her path, and Adeline says, "You can't force me to like you, you know."

"I didn't ask for this," her mother says. "I didn't cause this."

"Yeah, I know. You didn't do anything. You don't do anything. That's why he left. Who wouldn't leave you?"

Adeline feels the sting on the side of her face before she realizes that she's been slapped. She almost slaps her mother back, but the impulse comes too late, after the stunned second that shames her. Her mother doesn't move aside as Adeline walks past.

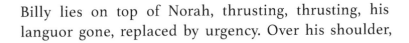

Billy lies on top of Norah, thrusting, thrusting, his languor gone, replaced by urgency. Over his shoulder, through the portal outside her bedroom window, Norah sees Adeline on Steve's porch.

Addy is sitting on the step, her backpack on the porch behind her. She is wearing a headlamp and reading a book. She smokes as she reads, and each time she takes a pull the glow of the cigarette lights her face, a red pulse before she disappears again into the shadow beneath the headlamp. When her cigarette is finished, she stubs it on the porch, unrolls her sleeping bag, crawls inside, and continues to read.

Billy thrusts faster, shudders, stiffens. Tears slide down Norah's temples and into her ears, and Billy looks concerned. "I'm sorry, Mrs. Caldwell," he says. He pulls away, slides off the bed and stumbles into his boxer shorts. "Are you okay? Did I hurt you?"

Norah wants to say go home, Billy. It's time for you to go home. But gravity has thickened, and the effort to speak seems so great. Billy puts on his shorts, pulls his t-shirt over his head, and stands beside the bed. He asks again if Norah is okay, and she rolls her eyes toward him. "Billy," she says, through the great weight of her pain. "Go home."

All night, Norah watches Addy sleep on Steve's porch, and as she watches, she remembers moments of Addy's life—her first latch onto Norah's breast, her first lost tooth, the summer they seemed to do nothing but eat popcorn and watch movies together. They're all there, these moments, in the air around Norah, Addy's entire life pulled into Norah's gravitational well.

Steve pulls into his driveway just before dawn. Norah doesn't know how late. She cannot turn to see her clock. As Steve walks up from his car he flaps his arms around his head, swatting away insects that Norah can't see.

When he notices the sleeping bag, he ignores the insects and leans in for a closer look. Sometime in the night, Adeline pulled the bag over her head against the cold, and Norah can see that Steve doesn't know who is there. Then he looks at the backpack and whispers, "Shit. Shit shit shit." For a long moment he doesn't move, and then he flinches as if stung. He flinches again, pulls off his jacket and whips it in circles around his head. Then he pulls his car key from his pocket, and as he stumbles to his car, Norah yells.

It is not a yell at all, however. It is a gurgling, pitiful sound, the sound that Addy must hear every time Norah speaks. But somehow the sound is enough. Steve turns toward Norah and squints into the darkness. Her bedroom light is off, and she imagines that he sees a circle of darkness layered on the darkness of his own night. She wonders if her light has always been off when the space between them folds. Or does he simply not look in her direction? He looks away now, toward Addy stirring in her sleep, and as he opens his car door it occurs to Norah that if she threw a stone hard enough, it might emerge from that layered darkness and strike him.

Adeline's mother is waiting at the dining-room table when Adeline returns from her night on her father's porch. Adeline leaves her headphones on, her mother's mouth moving, moving as Adeline walks past. Norah follows her into her room, her mouth still moving, moving as she stands over Adeline, who lies on her bed.

When Norah pulls the headphones off Adeline's ears the conversation is brief, beginning with Norah asking,

"Are you okay?" and ending with Adeline yelling up at the corner of the ceiling where Norah has retreated, "Thanks for ruining my life!" And for this too Adeline blames her mother. For making her say something so pathetic, so much like a cry for help. She will not speak again, will not move, will not look at that quivering thing on the ceiling. She does not flinch when her mother drops to the floor and crawls from the room. She does not flinch at the pounding of her mother's fist on the dining-room table. Does not flinch when she hears her mother's voice, "Answer the phone you son of a bitch! That's your daughter. You selfish son of a bitch!"

Adeline had seen her father drive away as she lay on his porch, had awoken at the closing of his car door. After she packed her sleeping bag she picked up rocks that ringed the weedy fringe that had once been her mother's flowerbed and threw them through every window on the first floor of his house.

When her mother leaves for work, Adeline pulls her phone from her backpack and calls her father. When he doesn't answer, she hits cancel, and then she presses call again. For an hour she does this. Call and cancel. Call and cancel. Twenty missed calls. Fifty. One hundred.

As she dials and redials, she thinks of the creature's words, *her* creature's words: "'There is love in me the likes of which you've never seen. There is rage in me the likes of which should never escape.'" She tells herself that when her father answers she will say this, and she will finish, "If I am not satisfied in the one, I will indulge in the other."

But when she finally lets the call go through to voicemail, she doesn't speak. Instead, she makes a sound that is supposed to be a laugh, a sound that she means to suggest both malice and dismissal but that instead sounds impotent and needy, and she hates him for this too.

She loads her phone's Facebook app, presses her mind away from the words upon which it is bent: "And what I now feel be no longer felt." She will not make this veiled declaration. She will not wonder if the post will get likes, or how many comments it will receive. She will not think of her parents seeing it, of what they'll say, how they'll grieve. She will not be dramatic.

When the app opens, she finds that she is not logged in. She types her username and password, and a message appears saying that the information is invalid. She retypes it, and the message reappears. She tries a third time, and then requests a password reset. When she enters her email address, she receives a message saying that there is no user associated with that address.

As she looks at the message, she does not feel angry. She feels no frustration, no self-pity. The twisted pain she had felt for so many days is gone. She's not hungry. She's not tired. Not anxious. She considers herself as from afar, and realizes that she feels nothing at all.

Norah's fingers encircle the grip of the handgun, a Browning Hill-Fire semiautomatic, she was told by the man who sold it to her. She is in bed again, propped up with two pillows behind her back. She learned of the gun show while she was at work, an advertisement for it printed on the newspaper that she lay across her counter as a blotter for cutting stems.

She spent several hours picking out the gun, her slowness in choosing not because she was particular, but because the show was in the air dome at the convention center, and she spent most of her time fighting her way down from the ballooned ceiling. Ever since she'd decided to buy the gun, she'd had a feeling of weightlessness, the result she thought of some chemical reaction, adrenaline or epinephrine, something in her body combining, combatting, canceling, somehow adding up to a net loss. She swam around the dome until she was close enough to a table to put the Browning into her hand, and at that instant she was standing on the ground. The weight of the gun shocked her at first, but as she held it and the room didn't rotate, didn't float out from beneath her, didn't rise up to smack her in the face, she realized that the weight was perfect, so perfect that as she turned the gun over in her hand and aimed it toward the table, she thought that this was the piece of herself she'd been missing all along.

Norah raises the gun now and points it toward her open bedroom window. Then she lowers it to the bed and lets her hand relax. She does this every few minutes. Before getting into bed, she drank three cups of coffee and swallowed half a dozen Sudafed. Even so, her fingers are growing stiff, and as she lifts the gun again her arm shakes. She wonders, as she lets her arm drop, if there is any way she'll be caught. She doesn't see how. She won't be at the scene of the crime. She will fire in her bedroom, and the bullet will arrive in Steve's living room, defying physics, the magic bullet that killed Kennedy.

Then the cosmic door is thrown open, and there sits Steve in his recliner chair, phone to his ear. "Yes," he says, "I'll be here." He stands, and Norah raises the pistol. The gun wavers, and she grips tighter, lines Steve in her sights. A second passes, and then two, and she hates him and hates him and doesn't shoot. The gun falls from her hand, and her arm drops to the bed.

Steve unbuckles his belt and lets his pants slide to his ankles. He kicks the pants into the air and catches them, and Norah wishes to god that she had shot him.

As he carries his pants to his bedroom, Norah's own bedroom door opens.

Adeline stands in the doorway. She looks blankly into Norah's eyes and then down her arm. There is no surprise when she sees the gun, only a head-tilt of curiosity before she steps forward, picks it up and points it at her own face. Norah tries to shout, "No," but there is no sound, and Adeline lowers the gun and walks with it out of the room.

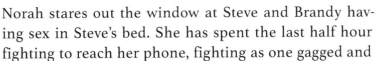

Norah stares out the window at Steve and Brandy having sex in Steve's bed. She has spent the last half hour fighting to reach her phone, fighting as one gagged and straightjacketed. She fights until she hears a knock on Steve's front door.

Then the world is still. Steve halted on top of Brandy. Brandy's fingernails arrested on Steve's back. The doorbell rings, and Steve puts his finger to his lips. He picks a towel up from the floor, wraps it around his waist and walks toward the door.

Norah's chest heaves. Her bedroom tilts in one direction, the window in another. Steve pulls the door open a crack, pokes his head through and says, "Who's there?"

Adeline stands under the porch lamp, arms at her sides.

"Is anyone there?" Steve asks, and Adeline raises the gun.

Gravity lets go of Norah, and the howl that has been circling within her breaks into the night. Steve turns toward the sound, and in his eyes there is shock, and then recognition, and then something like confusion, something like confession, like sorrow, remorse. It is an expression that erases time and distance and mass, and in the soundless vacuum that ensues there is only Norah and Steve. Norah reaches for him, and Steve puts his head in her lap. And he is sorry. He is so sorry.

Norah doesn't hear the gun's reports, but she sees the flashes—one, two, three—reflected in Steve's upturned eye.

There is a shift then, and Steve's eye is no longer his own. It is unmoored, a planet floating free. His pupil expands, swallows a continent of iris, and in the center of the void stands Adeline, a black gem in her father's eye. In miniature perfection she raises the gun to her temple. There is one more flash. A tiny spark. A supernova. And Norah understands that this is not happening. That this happened long ago. That it is yet to happen. That it is always happening. She understands that time is not a river. Norah is the river, drifting through the eternal sculpture of the all-that-is. If only she can figure out which muscle to flex, she thinks she might alter course. Might drift backward. Jump the banks. Live a thousand lives. A million realities.

The chasm in Steve's eye widens; Norah falls into it, and through his eye she sees herself as he first saw her, a nineteen-year-old girl sitting in a study carrel at their college library, her girlhood self reading a book, the same novel Steve holds in his hand as he walks by in his corduroy and tweed. When the girl looks up and smiles, Norah remembers the moment, remembers her feeling of recognition, something kindred in this man's eye. Steve nods and continues down the stacks, but with each step Norah can feel his growing conviction that in an ordered universe there are no chance meetings, no such thing as coincidence. He turns back, and as the girl places her bookmark between the pages of their shared novel they both feel certain that their story is already written, waiting only to be read.

SWEET MISERIES

"I found another one last night," Shelley says.

I'm in my office, my wife Shelley on the phone. It's my sixth week as assistant principal of Northside Middle School in Duluth, Minnesota. My office is next to the cafeteria, and the greasy sweetness of hamburger patties and tater tots drifts in a blue haze through the open window.

Until last spring, Shelley and I had taught sixth grade together in a small, suburban school outside Louisville, Kentucky. She had been taking night classes to earn her master's in education, and when I took the job in Duluth, she'd stayed behind to finish. We sold the house, put most of our belongings into storage, and each took an apartment. Shelley's is on the ground floor of a historic house in Old Louisville. Mine, a thousand miles away, is a loft in a brick warehouse on the shore of Lake Superior. The building is still being renovated, and I am its first tenant. The apartments around mine lie in varying states of completion, the buildings around mine derelict—the tip of a finger of rustbelt that reaches up from Chicago and Detroit, to the mothballed copper and steel mines, to the decaying piers that jut into Lake Superior like fallen skyscrapers.

"I hardly slept," Shelley says. "I kept hearing them. Walking around on all their little legs."

"They" are what Shelley's landlord calls Palmetto bugs—a pretty name for an oversized cockroach. Unlike their smaller cousins, however, they rarely infest homes, visiting instead as guests, one or two at a time, especially at this time of year as the weather cools in autumn. Despite their transient nature, Shelley had the apartment sprayed, and for the last week she's found one each morning on its back on the bathroom floor, legs waving in slow motion. They walk through it, the exterminator told her. The poison works its way up from their feet.

"This one was huge," Shelley says. "It must have been four inches long."

"It can't be four inches," I say.

She is home sick from school with the flu. I imagine her in her bathrobe, sitting on one end of the couch, feet pulled off the floor as she holds her thumb and finger in front of her, defining the length of the roach as she speaks.

The flu is sweeping through Northside Middle, too. It's an occupational hazard. Each winter we tiptoe through the fields of contagion that are our classrooms. We dope ourselves with hand sanitizer, cook our papers in microwave ovens.

Shelley and I began our romance during a flu epidemic five years ago. The outbreak occurred during the height of our female students' strawberry craze. Everything had been strawberries that fall. The girls wore strawberry-decal t-shirts, strawberry buttons on their backpacks, pink shoelaces with black dots that I think were supposed to be watermelon but that the girls thought were strawberry. They chewed strawberry gum, sucked on strawberry Ring Pops, ate pack after pack of pink strawberry Starbursts.

Shelley had been the new teacher in school. Her classroom was across the hall from mine, and we taught with our doors open. For weeks, I watched her chalk circles on her blackboard with an enormous wooden compass, listened to her voice—too low for words to reach me—as she milled back and forth along a line of students who stood at the board beneath towers of long division. I watched again and again the slit of her skirt fall open as she crouched to whisper into a child's ear.

For weeks, I held my best jokes until I saw her near her door, and I shouted them in her direction. I turned my chemistry set into a small pyrotechnic display, rallying my students to a countdown so that she would be sure to see it ignite. I transformed my lecture on continental drift into an ode to our unspoken desire, the convergence of two plates sliding inevitably closer on the smooth plastic of the asthenosphere. As I described the subduction zone, I saw her in the frame of her open door, her arm raised to the blackboard, an arrested piece of chalk in her fingers.

We had hardly spoken to each other before we made love. It was a Friday. After the students left, we both lingered in our rooms, puttering noisily, until I found myself at her door. I remember the conversation like this:

Me: Looks like you're getting a little cleaning done.
Shelley: You, too, I see.
Me: Just trying to contain the chaos.
Shelley: Chaos isn't such a bad thing.
Me: True. Children need a little chaos.
Shelley: Everybody needs a little chaos sometimes. (Beat.)
Don't they?

We closed the door between our classrooms for the first time that afternoon, and, there on her desk, surrounded by a faint aroma of strawberries, we collided like continents.

Two days after that meeting, I was out with the flu. The day I went home sick, the girls had all brought strawberry lip balm to school. It was everywhere, the petroleum of it stuck to their strawberry-Blow-Popped hands, invisible strawberry fingerprints pressed into the papers I had collected and stacked on the desk in front of me. Strawberry lip balm coated the tips of mittens and the fingers of gloves, transferred to that wet wool and nylon during applications at bus stops and on the playground. All afternoon, the gloves and mittens, drying on radiators, released a steaming blend of mildew and vaporized strawberry lip balm. That was the last thing I smelled before my sinuses swelled shut. For the next week, I was sure when I blew my nose that I smelled strawberry lip balm, sure that this was in fact what was trapped in my sinus cavities, melting from the heat of my fever. The sour sweetness has never completely left me. Whenever I have a head cold or a flu, it returns, a hint of it in the air, often before I recognize any symptoms. The scent of grossly sweet strawberries baking in wet wool on a hot radiator—my canary in the coal mine.

"I can't live with these bugs," Shelley says.

An exhaust fan rumbles to life somewhere on the roof, and a new wave of grill-smoke blows into my office, sending me into a fit of sneezing. I leave my desk and struggle to crank the tall window shut. The gears of the crank arm have seized, and I push hard on the handle. "You're obsessing over them, babe," I tell Shelley, the phone pinched against my shoulder, all my strength devoted to the handle that still doesn't turn. "It's the cold. They'll go away on their own when the weather turns."

"I don't care why they're here. I just want them gone."

I give up on the window, and as I walk back to my desk, the room wavers. My peripheral vision darkens, and I put my hand on the back of a chair. I take a deep breath, counting seconds as I inhale—one, two, three—and then wondering if three is right or if it should be four. "They'll hibernate, or whatever it is they do," I tell Shelley.

"What do they do?"

"They crawl into the ground and freeze," I say, though I don't know how they manage the winter. Flecks of black, like needle tips, float around my vision.

"You mean they're all around the house? Frozen in the ground? I feel like I'm surrounded."

"They die," I say. "I don't know."

"I wish you were here."

"You just want me there to take care of the bugs."

"I do," she says. "Lou and I aren't doing well, either." Lou is our dog, Lulu, whom we adopted from a shelter. Six weeks old and starving, she was listed as a terrier mix. Now grown, she is obviously pit bull, mixed with something large, rottweiler or mastiff. But despite the hundred-pound reality of her, we've never shed ourselves of the image of the small terrier—a Westie or a Scottie—that we thought she would become. "She pulls away every time I try to pet her," Shelley says. "I want her to sleep with me at night because of the bugs, but she won't."

Something in the right side of my chest flutters. Congestion, I think. I inhale again, searching the air for the scent of strawberries, but smelling only hamburgers and tater tots.

"Are you there?" Shelley asks.

"Yes," I say. "How are you feeling?"

"Better, I guess. It's a really bad flu. A third of our students are out with it. If it gets any worse, they'll close the school."

"It's here, too," I say. "Spreading like crazy." My vision begins to open, the black flecks floating away. "I have to go," I say. "They're serving lunch in a few minutes."

"Okay. Call me tonight."

I hear Lulu's dog tags jingle.

"She's letting me pet her," Shelley says. "I'm going to try to get her to stay on the couch with me. She'll be my guard dog. Won't you, Lou?"

"Gotta go, babe. Love you."

"Call me."

I first felt the dizziness last night, the stars swimming in my vision as I walked up the stairs to my apartment. The elevator is not yet installed in my building, and my apartment is on the top floor. Four flights of stairs after a long day on my feet, I thought at the time. Understandable. But I felt it again this morning, a shortness of breath as I walked from my car to my office.

I wait at my desk until I'm sure the sensation has passed. Then I put on my sports coat and leave for the cafeteria. "I think I may be coming down with the flu," I say to the secretary on my way out.

"You and everyone else," she says, without looking up from her computer screen.

Toward the end of lunch, after half an hour of walking among tables, mingling with the children in the cafeteria, I once again feel lightheaded. Just as I overhear a girl say, "He showed *it* to me," darkness creeps into the edges of my vision.

The girl is wearing sparkling pink lipstick, her blonde bangs teased into a poof that rides on her forehead. Two girls sit close on either side of her, a third girl one seat removed, looking at the table. "It was *so* gross," the blonde-haired girl continues. "It looked like a turtle. He wanted me to touch it. Yeah, right."

I put my hand on the girl's shoulder, pushing harder than I'd meant as I steady myself. A black speck loops in front of my eyes and disappears. The girl stiffens at my touch, and then smiles at the girls around her.

"Hello, ladies," I say. "How was lunch?"

"Fine, Mr. Spencer," the blonde-haired girl says. They all look up at me, and I see that the girl who sits apart has a birthmark on her face. It's brown and raised, half of it backed up under her ear, huddled there like a timid mouse. As soon as I notice, she tilts her head down and pulls her hair over it. The bell rings for recess, and the girls run off, the one with the birthmark following behind. They all look back at once, and I think they must be talking about me.

I fall into the chair that the girl with the birthmark has vacated, and I wait to catch my breath. It's the flu, I tell myself, inhaling again, searching the air for the scent of strawberries. It's only the flu.

Tom and I took an asbestos safety course before we started the roofing job. We were both twenty-three years old, though Tom seemed older. He was recently married, and he and Tracy had a baby on the way. I was single, living in a popup trailer that I moved between job sites. This job was a tear-off and re-roof. We'd be removing asbestos tiles that sprawled over six gables, across eight-thousand square-feet of house. It would take us the rest of the summer and would be my last job with Tom before I went away to school. I had recently begun tutoring my niece in math and English, and I'd found that I liked it. The lessons had begun informally, accidentally, over Thanksgiving weekend, but I quickly began to look forward to them, began to think up math games and English scavenger hunts as I hung drywall and plumbed toilets.

The kid who ran the asbestos class was nineteen, and he loved the stuff. He sat at Tom's kitchen table in ripped jeans and a black Metallica t-shirt, and he placed on the table in front of him three rocks covered in asbestos. They were sealed in plexiglass cubes, little stones with heads of white hair that looked almost like cotton, except that the fibers were straight and sharp, half-inch needles. If you pressed your finger on them, they'd slip right into you, no problem. He told us how the ancient Greeks had named it—asbestos, "unquenchable." He pronounced *unquenchable* as if it had a capital *U*, as if it were the title of a new Metallica album.

He told us how the Greeks had mined it, had woven it into cloth. He told us how the ancient Persians had wrapped their arms and legs in it and dipped them into fire to impress their friends. The Egyptians had used it as wicks in their sepulchral lamps. The Hittites wove it into shrouds and wrapped the bodies of their kings in it, the silverwhite blankets cradling their remains so they wouldn't get lost in the coals of the funeral pyre.

He talked about asbestos like Tom talked about DeWalt and Milwaukee power tools. Asbestos was this kid's Alpha and his Omega. It was his death metal band, his semi-auto handgun, and his muscle car all rolled into one, and when he talked about it, he was somewhere else—on a back road at night, cresting a hill at a hundred miles an hour with the Black Sabbath cranked, a bottle of Jim Beam between his legs, and the headlights turned off.

Our final exam was to test the seal on the carbon-filter gas masks we'd be working in. We stood together beneath the exhaust vent in Tom's bathroom and bowed our heads as if in prayer, while the kid waved a burning smudge stick beneath our chins, the noxious smoke rolling over the plastic that covered our mouths. "You better hope those masks seal," he said from behind his own. "This smoke is wicked. Last guy I tested puked. In his mask!"

I sit in the cafeteria until all the children have left for recess, until one of the workers comes over to wipe down the table. When I return to my office, the secretary reminds me of Friday's meeting with the PTA. This will be our first meeting, and I am to write a speech. I stay late to work on it, but I spend most of my time monitoring my breathing, convincing myself alternately that I am suffocating and that I am imagining the whole thing.

The sun is setting as I drive home, and by the time I dip into the parking garage, I leave behind only a hint of crimson lining the bottom of a single cloud. Mine is the only car in the garage, and the thunk of my closing door echoes around the vast hangar, my footsteps pinging like sonar off the distant concrete walls.

Inside the building, the hallway light fixtures have not yet been wired, and I navigate by the red glow of exit signs. As I walk past the elevator on my way to the stairs, I see that the doors have been installed. I press the up button. It lights, and I hear a soft whirring, but when the bell dings the doors open into an empty shaft.

I turn to the stairwell, and by the third-floor landing I'm winded. I pull myself up the last flight and rest in the doorway.

A powder of white drywall dust, red in the glow of the exit signs, coats the hallway carpet. The dust is broken by a network of footprints, and I see this morning's impressions of my narrow dress shoes coming at me from the end of the hall, their faint marks trampled by the soles of work boots.

I step into my apartment and slip off my dusty shoes. At first glance, the apartment looks as unfinished as the rest of the building, but the look is intentional, the renovation meant to retain the warehouse feel. The exterior walls are brick, the ceiling open, piping and ductwork snaking along the joists.

I heat a frozen dinner, something purporting to be Asian—broccoli and chicken in a sweet sauce. I pour a glass of red wine from a box and use it to wash down four Advil. Then I sit at my table, open my laptop, and slide it near the window. The building manager laughed when I asked about internet access, but I found that if my laptop is at the right angle, I can catch a wifi signal from a network called Shangri-La. I don't know where this faint signal is coming from, don't know where Shangri-La could possibly be in the defunct industrial park that surrounds me.

I am nearing the end of my second glass of wine by the time I work up the nerve to abandon my half-hearted attempt at the PTA speech, and instead type "asbestos" into a search engine. I avoid the medical pages and go instead for history.

First, I read about magic. I learn that although the Greeks named it Unquenchable, for its fire-resistance, the Romans called it Amiantus, Undefiled, for its seemingly magical resistance to soiling. Pliny the Elder saw it as a talisman, writing that asbestos "affords protection against all spells, especially those of the Magi."

Then, despite my avoidance of medical pages, my reading turns to health. I learn that Sappho and Herodotus both noted that slaves who mined and wove asbestos commonly suffered from a disease of the lungs. I don't learn why, but after these early reports, a historical quiet ensues, millennia of dead air, until 1906, when Denis Auribault, a French factory inspector, publishes an article in *Le Bulletin de l'Inspection du Travail*. Auribault concluded that fifty workers at an asbestos spinning factory in Paris had died of chalicosis, a disease common in stonecutters, caused by the inhalation of ground stone dust. Twenty years later, British pathologist W. E. Cooke wrote in *British Medical Journal* of a woman named "Maggie" who died at age thirty-three, after having worked in an asbestos factory since the age of thirteen. "Atmospheric conditions were occasionally so bad," Cooke wrote, "that workers in her particular room could not see each other." Her lungs were sent to London, where x-rays showed extensive fibrosis. "They are of a woody texture," the coroner wrote, "much like the rind of a coconut."

I don't know how many glasses of wine I've drunk, but at some point I move from the glow of my computer to my bed, where I lie on my back and think of Tom's son, whom he named Tom Junior—Tommy. I received an invitation to Tommy's high-school graduation two years ago. I didn't go. I remember when Tom told me he would name his son after himself. He had just handed me my last paycheck, along with a five-hundred-dollar bonus. Hush money, I suspected. And I was right. We never spoke of the job again. Tom Junior, I thought, as I folded the bills and put them into my pocket. Tom Two. A second chance.

Before I fall asleep, I notice a pipe above my bed, wrapped in paper-backed insulation. The paper is yellowed, and I think that it is not part of the new construction, but a remnant of the original infrastructure. At a junction in the pipe, a spidery tuft of insulation blooms from a crack in the paper.

I remember that I had turned my ringer off that afternoon, that I hadn't called Shelley. I think of her on her bed with Lulu, hiding from the bugs. I wish she were with me. I want to make love to her. I want a baby. I desperately want a baby.

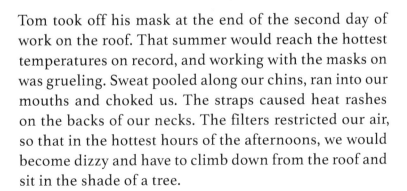

Tom took off his mask at the end of the second day of work on the roof. That summer would reach the hottest temperatures on record, and working with the masks on was grueling. Sweat pooled along our chins, ran into our mouths and choked us. The straps caused heat rashes on the backs of our necks. The filters restricted our air, so that in the hottest hours of the afternoons, we would become dizzy and have to climb down from the roof and sit in the shade of a tree.

On the second afternoon, our masks raised to our fore-heads for a water break, Tom said, "Screw it," and pulled the mask from his head and flung it at the base of the tree.

According to the kid who did the asbestos safety course, we didn't need to wear the masks at all. "This shit isn't even friable," he'd said on our first morning of work. He was sitting in the grass, hunched over a micro-scope. He wasn't wearing a mask. "There aren't even two fibers per. You guys are clear," he said. "It's the insulation jobs you have to worry about. You need full body suits for that. Forced air. Decontamination show-ers. You name it."

For three days after Tom shed his, I wore my mask, tipping it up every few minutes to let the sweat drain from my chin. Each day was hotter than the last, the humidity higher. The mask hung from my neck as I ate lunch that third day, and before I climbed back up to the roof I pulled it off and tossed it at the base of the tree.

For a week I worked without the mask. As we tore off the asbestos tiles, and the job grew dirtier, the dust thicker, I thought of other jobs I had done with Tom. Who knows what kind of shit we'd been into, I thought. Shit we didn't even realize we were into. I thought about basements and crawl spaces, black mold and solder smoke. I spent hours on the roof imagining myself in these other places, the worst places.

Then, at the end of that week, I peeled my t-shirt from my body as I always did at day's end, and I flipped it in the air to dislodge the debris. The fabric snapped, and a thick cloud of glass-like fibers shimmered pris-matically against the sunset, a miniature rainbow that hung in the air for a second before it broke apart and drifted weightlessly away.

I wake with half a glass of wine on my nightstand and nine calls from Shelley showing on my phone. She left three messages. The first at 6:45 p.m.: "Babe, where are you? You said you'd call. Call me." The next at ten o'clock: "You forgot about me. Lou and I are going to bed. I'm afraid to turn off the lights. They're going to be crawling all over the floor." The phone brushes against something, and I hear her hand patting the mattress. "Come on, Lulu," she says. "Come sleep with Mommy." The last message came at three a.m., Shelley's whisper, amplified, I think, by her hands cupped around the phone: "Oh, babe." she says. "They're everywhere."

I call her during the hour before lunch, my quiet hour, the kids too concerned about missing recess to cause much trouble. By the end of recess, I will have a line of kids sitting in wooden chairs outside my door.

Shelley answers the phone with, "Where were you?"

I apologize for not calling, tell her about the ringer.

"We had a terrible night," she says. "I just don't know how I'm going to survive these bugs."

"You'll survive."

"There were two of them on their backs on the bathroom floor, their legs moving all together like that. Ugh. They have so many legs."

"There's nothing you can do about it," I say. "It'll pass."

"I have to do something. The landlord has to seal up the house. There must be holes."

"You can't seal a house from insects."

"He could caulk it."

"You can't caulk a whole house. Bugs get in. They come in from anywhere. Through the ductwork. The pipes."

"The ductwork? You mean the heating vents? Oh my god. The vents are in my ceiling. Above my bed. I can't sleep here."

"Babe, you're just getting yourself worked up."

"I found those two in the middle of the night. I could have stepped on them. But I always turn on the lights now before I step anywhere. I know them. I do. I knew they'd be there, and there they were, right beside each other. Just lying on their backs like that."

I have been feeling bad all day. I'm hungover, winded. Twice, as I met with the principal this morning to discuss my PTA speech, my vision began to waver as I ran out of breath, and I had to stop talking. I nodded instead, and tightened my lips as if I were deep in thought. "Just so you know," he said as I left his office, "those women can smell BS a mile off."

Since then, I've spent so much time concentrating on my breathing that it has become mechanical, and at times I wonder if I'm causing my own shortness of breath, a sort of reverse hyperventilation. I think about telling Shelley, but I'm not sure what to tell her. That I think I have the flu? That I'm afraid for my life?

"Babe," I say. But I don't know how to continue. I inhale—one last searching breath to convince myself that this is not my imagination—and I smell them. Strawberries. Overripe, cooked, pungent. I laugh, or I sigh, a dumbfounded huff. A funny. An incredible relief. "I have the flu," I say.

"Why do you sound happy about it?"

I laugh again. I feel tears. "I guess I am."

"I'm going to have to move out," she says. "I think Lou ate one of them. I wanted her to get them, but I didn't think about it."

"Babe, I have the flu."

"I know. I'm sorry. I am. But do you think the bug will make her sick?"

"Babe."

"It's not just a bug, you know. It's a poisoned bug."

Shelley tells me to go home, to drink lots of fluids, to get rest. She reminds me to leave my ringer on this time. I hang up the phone and take a deep breath. The strawberries are still there. I feel an irritation in the back of my throat, pressure in my sinuses. My chest feels tight, and I cough—dry, but with a hint of congestion, I'm sure. Almost sure. By morning, I think, it will be worse.

I leave my office and join the flow of fifth and sixth graders heading to lunch. The blonde girl with the pink lipstick walks ahead of me with her friends, the girl with the birthmark again two steps behind.

The scent of strawberries grows stronger as I enter the cafeteria. Stronger as I approach the food line. And there they are, cooked into an oatmeal-crumb-covered mush that I'm sure the cooks call strawberry cobbler.

"How could you forget to have your phone on?" I ask. I'm in my office, standing by the window, the phone to my ear. School has just let out. I've been trying to reach Shelley all afternoon. The rain from the night before hasn't let up. Everything is damp, and my breath comes heavier than ever.

"You're the one who forgot your phone last night," Shelley says.

"And you threw a fit."

"I didn't throw a fit."

"You're right," I say. The window is open a crack and a dull static of rain sounds from the four-square courts. "Let's drop it. I feel like hell."

"So do I. I called the landlord again. He said he couldn't seal the house. I told him he needed to send another exterminator. They aren't dying anymore. I think they're getting immune."

"They can't get immune. That takes generations."

"Well, they're not dying. By the time I got up the nerve to flush one, it was gone."

"You just need to relax," I say. "They'll leave on their own."

"That's easy for you to say. You don't have to deal with them."

"If I were there, I'd say the same thing."

"But you're not here."

"No," I concede. "I'm not."

Above the sound of rain, I hear the squeak of a rubber boot against the pavement outside my window. It's the girl with the birthmark, standing under the roof overhang. She's wearing a black raincoat.

"How's your flu?" I ask Shelley.

"Better. I'm going to work tomorrow. How are you feeling?"

"I'm okay," I say. "Maybe I don't have the flu at all." The girl holds out her hand, catching the fat drops of rain that fall from the roof. "Are we going to make it?" I ask.

"Make what? What are you talking about?"

"I'm looking down the tunnel of this year, and it just seems to go on and on. I can't see the end of it."

The girl steps out from under the eave. She tilts her head back, lets the rain fall onto her closed eyes, onto the exposed length of her birthmark.

"I know," Shelley says.

"What do you mean you know?" I ask.

"I feel the same way."

The girl opens her eyes and blinks up into the rain. A rivulet of water slides down her cheek and curves around the birthmark's raised contour. She wipes the water away, her fingertips caressing the brown softness there from end to end.

"I want to have a baby," I say.

"A baby? What brought this up?"

"Why not? Why not have a baby?"

"Well, for one thing, I'm a thousand miles away. I don't think your swimmers are that strong."

"I'm serious."

"So am I."

"Let's have a baby. Let's really have a baby."

"Tell me why you're bringing this up right now."

The girl ducks back under the eave and leans against the brick wall. I close my eyes and inhale a shallow breath. When I open my eyes, the girl is gone.

"Just before it's too late," I say. "Let's have a baby before it's too late."

"You should have thought of this before you left me here."

"I didn't leave you there," I say.

"Well, we were here together. Then you went away, and I'm still here. I call that leaving."

"Don't do this."

"What am I doing?"

I hear Lulu's tags jingle. She's pressing herself against Shelley's legs, I'm sure, as she does when we argue. "Do you remember when we got together?" I ask. "When I was so sick, and you came over every day after school?

Even though I told you not to. And we made love. And I was so sweaty. I can't imagine what I must have smelled like. I was so sure you would get sick, too."

"But I didn't."

"No," I say. "You didn't."

The phone is quiet for a moment before Shelley says, "I should really go. I'm back at school tomorrow, and I have a ton of work to do."

"I miss you, Shell," I say.

Lulu's tags jingle.

"I said I miss you, babe."

"I know. I miss you, too."

I sit at my desk, listening to the rain for half an hour after I hang up the phone. When I come out of my office, a scattering of students are still in the hallway, making their way from their after-school activities to the front doors, where their parents will be waiting in idling cars. A long, panoramic mirror painted with life-size images of children spans one wall of the foyer, and standing between two painted boys, looking at herself, is the blonde-haired girl.

She wears a leotard, a flowered sarong wrapped around her waist. She tilts her head from side to side, pouts her lips, picks at her teased bangs. Then she turns her back to the mirror and twists around to look at her backside.

Just as she sees me through the mirror, someone calls, "Samantha," and I turn to see a woman of about my age standing just inside one of the glass front doors. Her hair is bleached, her bangs teased like the girl's. She chews gum, and in one hand, propped just outside the door, she holds a cigarette. "Get your ass over here, Princess," she says. "Carriage is leaving."

Samantha looks from her mother to me. She blushes deeply, her cheeks two irregular blotches of crimson. I wonder, as she walks through the rain to her mother's minivan, if her blush is from shame or from hatred, and whom she hates most at that moment.

I am lying on my stomach in my bed. I don't know what time it is. The pale silver of a distant security light reflects in the rain-spattered windows of my apartment. I have finished my box of wine.

The phone rings. I don't answer it.

My chest aches dully, and I tell myself that it is only from the hard mattress. I should roll onto my back, but I don't. I run my mind around the contour of my pain, memorize it, catalogue it to mull over later.

The phone rings again, and I remember the day Tom's son was born, the trumpet blast of Tom's voice on the phone. I remember Shelley and me on the desk in her classroom, the blast of that collision. I remember, too late, the PTA speech that I was supposed to have given that evening.

The phone stops ringing, and the apartment is quiet for a moment before the phone rings again.

I don't know for how many minutes or hours Shelley has been hitting redial. I imagine her on her bed, the ringing phone in her hand, blankets pulled up to her chin. I imagine the roaches, big as ears, welling up from her shower drain, pushing through the heat vents and fanning across the ceiling above her bed. I sneeze, and I am overwhelmed with the scent of rotting strawberries. Dimly, I realize that I have a fever. A thick, wet cough breaks from my chest, and though I know these berries are not real, I taste them all the same. I cling to them, my sweet miseries, just as I imagine they must cling to their fetid vines, all of us afraid that if we let go, we may lose our way, and drift off to heaven.

PLASTIC'
FANTASTIC'

My wife was standing with our two girls, sifting through a table of books—twenty-five cents per paperback, a dollar per hardcover—when I saw the Han Solo and Princess Leia figures lying together in a cardboard box. Two thin, plastic people, the original 1970s versions.

We had argued through dinner, the same argument as always, some small negligence—on this day, a forgotten loaf of bread—opening the door to a litany of past offenses, little injustices that fell like dominoes, trailing back nearly to the day we met. The evening was warm, the first summery day that early June, and we had taken our Sunday walk despite the argument, and had stopped at this yard sale. The homeowners were closing down, the father and his sons carrying tables into the garage—lamps and dishes and small kitchen appliances balanced on their tops. I had been hoping to find some quirky yard-sale trinket that I could hold up to my wife, something we would laugh weakly about, a little talisman to ward off the fighting for another day. When I found the Star Wars figures, I had not, however, thought of them as charms for my wife and me, but for a boy I once knew, "a long time ago, in a galaxy far, far away." They were in perfect condition, as fresh and bright as when they were newly minted decades earlier, as fresh and bright as those Jody held in his fists on a winter night in 1978, a night that I hadn't known I'd remembered, that I hadn't known I'd forgotten, one night among so many lost in the shadow of my parents' divorce.

I was ten years old. My brother, Peter, was thirteen, Jody, seven. We were sitting on a yellow shag carpet in front of the wood stove at my father's house, an old farmhouse perched on a bluff above a lonely stretch of Lake Michigan coastline. The wind blew day and night from the lake, the scattering of trees around the house beaten down from it, the sound of it forever in my ears.

My father and Jody's mother had just gone to bed. Marcie didn't spend the night often, never before with her son. They'd been trapped on this night by a storm, the road drifted shut, snow sliding like waves across the field in front of our house. Peter had suggested a slumber party, and our father had brought three army-issue sleeping bags, rolled and cinched with belts, down from an eaves closet. While Peter and I staked out our territory, Jody looked uncertainly at his bag. His mother unbuckled the belt for him, the bag flopped open, and he crinkled his nose against the earthy scent of dry-rotting canvas. His mother unzipped the zipper partway and folded the fabric back so that it made a triangle. She went upstairs and returned with pillows, fluffed one and laid it on the exposed lining of Jody's sleeping bag. She kissed him on the lips, then on the forehead, and he watched her follow my father through the kitchen and into the bedroom. She blew him one last kiss, closed the door, and Jody joined us at the wood stove.

The cast iron doors of the stove were open, and a log smoldered in the fire, a few weak flames licking the circumference of charred bark, reflecting dully off our cheeks and throwing hollow shadows over our eyes. The storm rattled the double-hung windows, echoed down the metal stovepipe. Jody flinched at every gust, looked at the windows, looked at us.

"Do you want to hear a ghost story?" Peter asked.

We had first met Jody two months earlier, when our father had taken us to Marcie's house, a doublewide trailer that he called a modular home. The house was newly delivered from the factory, and it sat alone in a mowed patch of field on the edge of town. We had gone there to build a tool shed in the backyard for rakes and garden hoses and Marcie's push mower. We arrived just after sunup, and the field shone golden in the late-autumn sun, grasses as high as my chest walling the carved square of Marcie's yard. My father drove our Chevy Impala around the house and parked in back, the prefabricated parts of the toolshed in cardboard boxes tied to the car's roof.

We found Jody sitting at a table in the kitchen. He wore a Star Wars t-shirt—Luke Skywalker with his lightsaber held in both hands over his head, the Death Star in the background. The shower was running, and my father ducked into the bathroom. He poked his head back out and said to Jody, "Your mother says to show the boys your room." I said I was hungry, and my father told us we'd have pancakes before we started on the shed. He stayed in the bathroom, and Peter and I followed Jody down a narrow hallway to the back of the house. As we passed the closed bathroom door, I heard Marcie laugh. He must be tickling her, I thought.

The floor creaked as we walked down the hall, and when I bumped Jody's bedroom door with my shoulder, it swung into the wall with a hollow thud. I had never been inside a modular home, a home with floors that flexed beneath my feet, with doors light as cardboard, trim and doorknobs made of plastic. And I had never been in a bedroom like Jody's.

His bed frame was shaped like a race car, his sheets printed with cartoon scenes from Speed Racer. His wallpaper was Battlestar Galactica. His carpet was bright red shag, his ceiling cornflower blue, pasted with planets and stars that I was sure glowed in the dark. And spanning one wall were half a dozen shelves filled with toys—toys made of plastic, toys that took batteries and came with accessories, toys that seemed a world away from our Lincoln Logs, board games, and books. He had the Justice League superheroes and their Hall of Justice playset. He had the entire Star Trek crew and the Enterprise bridge. He had a dozen G.I. Joes, Planet of the Apes, Action Jackson, Evel Knievel and the Super Stunt Cycle, X-wings and TIE Fighters, and the Death Star complete with trash compactor. He had Stretch Armstrong, Stretch Monster, and Stretch Spiderman and Hulk, which I hadn't even known existed. And in one corner, on his red-white-and-blue dresser, was an RCA color TV.

Jody's action figures seemed a better fit for this house than did real, flesh and blood people. They seemed a better fit for Marcie's car, too, which had amazed Peter and me when we first saw it. It was a Toyota Corolla, a new breed of automobile, with a plastic interior, plastic bumpers and grill. It squeaked when it hit bumps. Our car rattled over bumps, stank of raw gas and mildewed floorboards. Peter called their car the Plastic Fantastic, and for years that's how I thought of this boy and his mother: The Plastic Fantastics.

Jody and Marcie. Ken and Barbie.

Jody was small and perfectly proportioned, without any outstanding features, but with a beauty that came from his symmetry, from his flawless glowing skin, from his thick shiny hair, cut into the same perfect bowl that Peter and I saw on the heads of children in the TV commercials for the toys that we saw in Jody's bedroom. And Marcie looked the perfect TV mom, a short bob of sprayed hair, a beauty mark on her cheek in the exact same spot as Florence Henderson's.

If my brother and father and I had been on TV, our show would have been about survival. It would star a bearded father whose eyes never seemed to rest and two rail-thin boys, hair uncut since our mother left six months earlier, clothes half a size too small. Our show would be *Land of the Lost* or *Swiss Family Robinson*, without the good looks and affable personalities. Without the dialogue. When I see our family photographs from that time, I think we look like the windblown trees on that hill, like the ancient fence posts scattered in haphazard lines between one forgotten field and the next.

A wash of snow and wind passed over our father's house, and the small flames flared in the fireplace. Jody said he didn't want to hear a ghost story, and I suggested we put another log on the fire.

"We could turn on the lights," Jody said. "I brought toys we could play with."

"We can't turn on the lights," Peter said. "Dad might come out."

Jody looked at me. I looked at Peter. Then we all turned our heads toward our father's bedroom on the far side of the kitchen, where a flickering orange glow reached out from beneath the closed door and spread across the black and white linoleum.

"He won't see," Jody said. "The door's closed."

"That's candle light," Peter said. "He can't take artificial lights after midnight. They burn his eyes."

Earlier that day, while my father and Marcie had attempted to dig out the driveway, Peter and I had taken Jody into our father's bedroom, where Peter tried to convince him that our father was a werewolf. Our father was hairy enough, his body covered in an unbroken layer of fur, a mane of hair running up his spine. And on his new waterbed was the evidence of his barbaric feasts. Peter reached into one corner of the bed frame and lifted the free end of a leather strap. "This is where he ties up his victims," he said.

Our father had bought the waterbed while Peter and I were visiting our mother, who had moved back to her hometown. She was living with her sister and taking nursing classes at the community college. In two years, she told us as she put us on the Greyhound back to our father's, she would have her license, would buy a house, and we could live with her. Peter told her we were fine where we were, and when she reached to touch his head he pulled away. "Okay, honey," she told him. "That's okay."

While we'd been away, our father had also bought himself a new wardrobe. When we returned from our mother's, he met us at the bus stop wearing flare-legged jeans and a polyester paisley shirt, unbuttoned to the bottom of his sternum, a gold chain nesting in the thick mat of his chest hair. At home, he showed off the new yellow shag carpet in the living room. Then he brought us into his remodeled bedroom, a room in some ways similar to Jody's. He had put in a thick burgundy carpet, several shades darker than Jody's red. He had a color television, a Betamax videotape player beside it. Instead of a race-car bed, he had the new waterbed. Instead of Speed Racer sheets, he had burgundy satin sheets, covered with a faux bearskin bedspread. Instead of stars on his ceiling, he had mirrors. He smiled as I lay on the waterbed and looked at myself reflected in the ceiling, my skinny body in cut-off jeans and a Coca Cola t-shirt. I waved my arms and legs, watching my knees and elbows move on the ceiling, and feeling some charge of excitement at the touch of the smooth satin on my skin.

My father had plastic toys in his new bedroom, too. I went often into his room to lay on those satin sheets and look into the mirrors, and I found the toys in one of the nightstand drawers, two oblong, colored objects—one hard and baby blue, the other soft and pink. I thought of them as rockets, though I knew they weren't rockets. The hard one had a knurled dial on its base, and when I twisted it, the rocket vibrated. I held it against my neck. "Take me to your leader," I said, my voice quavering with the vibrations. "I come in peace."

Peter had been the one to find the leather straps tied to the four corners of our father's bed.

"What are they for?" I asked, when he showed me.

"For tying people down," he said.

"Why?"

"Why do you think, dummy?"

I imagined myself strapped by my wrists and ankles, my father tickling me like he used to in the evenings on the living-room floor, when Peter would help to hold me down and our mother would warn that someone was going to get hurt.

"I don't know," I said to Peter. "Tickle torture?"

"Yeah, tickle torture," he said. "Tickle torture with Marcie's plastic fantastic."

Jody had stopped two steps into the bedroom as Peter held up the leather strap and told him about our father's other victims. All women. All with children who now lived in orphanages. "See these red sheets?" Peter said. "They used to be white." Jody said he didn't believe it, but I knew it was true. The sheets had been white as long as I could remember, and the bedspread beige, a wedding gift to our parents from our grandmother. Jody asked me if it were true, and I looked at Peter and didn't answer. "You're such a fucking baby," Peter said to me. For the next hour, Jody sat by the living-room window and watched the figures of our parents, the primary colors of their winter gear appearing and disappearing in the whitewash of snow, as they lost the battle with the storm.

Marcie appeared from her bathroom, from a door as narrow as any I had ever seen in a house, and she joined my father in the kitchen. He was just finishing up a stack of pancakes, our breakfast before we went to work on the shed. When he set the platter on the table, we saw that he had poured the batter into the shapes of animals—turtles, bears, Mickey Mouse. "I don't know why everybody thinks they have to be round," he said as he forked a pancake onto his plate. Then he looked with comic intensity at his pancake and added, "Oops, I think I gave the horse a hard-on." He laughed like Goofy, and Jody laughed with him.

Jody used syrup to make eyes and mouths and stripes on the pancakes. He bounced on his seat as he ate, and he chattered on about which animals Peter and I had on our plates, which parts we should eat first.

The morning was cold, and the thick field-stubble that was Marcie's yard was wet with dew. As we unpacked the aluminum strips that would frame the shed, my fingers grew red and stiff. Marcie brought me a pair of her gloves, flesh-colored and smelling of her rose perfume and the talcum scent of her makeup. They stretched over my fingers like nylons. Peter said he didn't need any gloves, and he and my father worked barehanded, bolting together the lengths of frame as I held them in place. Once the frame was finished, we stepped back to look at our work. The sun was high over the field now, warm on our faces, drying the yard. The frame glinted in the sunlight, an Erector Set skeleton of a house.

"I bet this is the same stuff their house is built with," Peter said.

"Watch it, my man," our father said.

"Well it's such a piece of crap," Peter said. "I'm waiting to step right through the floor."

My father wrapped his hand around the back of Peter's neck. "I might marry that lady someday," he said. "Don't piss in your pool, Son."

"This isn't my pool," Peter said and pulled himself away from our father's hand.

"You're damn right there," our father said. "So better yet, don't piss in my pool."

Marcie brought out coffee for Peter and my father. I'd never seen Peter drink coffee, and I watched his face sour as he took his first sip.

"What are you looking at?" he said.

My father laughed and swiped a hand over Peter's head. "Come on, let's get the sides up."

By noon, we had finished attaching the sides, Peter and I holding the plastic panels in place, while our father screwed them to the frame with sheet-metal screws. We ate peanut butter and jelly sandwiches in the backyard, and then as we started on the roof Jody joined us. Marcie had put him in a white down vest and green mittens, and as he walked toward us, his vest blinding in the sunlight, I looked at my own jacket. It had been powder blue when my mother had me try it on at the end-of-season sale at J.C. Penney that spring. But now the coat was more earth-toned than blue, the polyester fibers embedded with dirt from carrying firewood.

As Jody stood in the yard, Peter and I handed strips of vinyl roofing material to my father who stood on a stepladder inside the shed. My father had taken off his shirt, despite the chill of coming winter, and Jody stared at his hairy torso, displayed over the tops of the walls.

"Come here, Jody," my father said. "Why don't you help me with the roof."

Jody looked up at my father, who might have been naked for all he could see from where he stood, and shook his head.

"Come on," my father said. "I won't bite."

Jody looked longingly back at the house and then stepped into the shed. He reappeared above the walls, standing near the top rung of the ladder with my father below him. I handed a vinyl strip to Peter, and he swung it into place, one end down at the eave, the other resting on the ridge.

"See that hole there?" my father asked Jody, pointing to the last strip they'd attached. Jody nodded. "See this nipple?" my father asked, and he pinched a round, flanged tab between his finger and thumb.

Jody looked at my father's face when he heard the word *nipple*.

"When I get the piece in place, you line up that nipple with the hole and push it until you feel it snap together."

"I want to get down now," Jody said.

"You can do it. Just reach up there. I've got you."

"I want to get down," Jody repeated.

"Oh, for Christ's sake," my father said. "Just do it." He held the piece in place and Jody reached up and pushed.

When the pieces snapped together, they pinched the tip of Jody's mitten between the slats. He shrieked and jerked his hand out of his mitten. My father lost his balance, and he and Jody slid down the ladder and fell against the wall. I heard the pop of screws as one of the vinyl panels tore away from the frame. Jody jumped up and ran out of the shed. In the middle of the yard he turned around, his white vest streaked with dirt, the corner of one pocket torn. My father stepped out of the shed, and Jody ran into the house.

I didn't want a ghost story either. I didn't want to talk about our father being a werewolf. I pulled the fire poker from the ash bin, prodded the smoldering log, and the fire flamed back to life.

"Once upon a time," Peter said, "There were two little boys, seven and ten, home for the night with the babysitter. It was getting cold, and they had only one log left for the fire."

Jody and I looked at the last unburned log, a paper-birch that lay on the brick base surrounding the wood stove. I suggested we put it on the fire, but Peter thought that it would spoil the mood.

I dropped the poker into the bin, and Peter told Three Knocks, a ghost story that he and I told each other often. He told an especially brutal version, dragging his knuckles on the end table each time he said, "knock . . . knock . . . knock." He fashioned the house in the story after our own, and added a winter storm raging outside as it was that night. He gave the marauding murderer a beard and covered him in hair, like our father, and he gave the babysitter a mole on her cheek, "a mole so ugly that the two boys were afraid to look at it." At the end of the story, the babysitter stumbled into the house with an axe embedded in her skull and a bloody hole where her mole had been gouged out. Jody pressed his body against my hip, and I pushed him away, told him to get off me.

When Peter's story was finished, Jody listed his favorite cartoons and his favorite breakfast cereals, his favorite Disney characters and his favorite rides at Disney World, where he had gone with his mother that summer. His lists were bright and colorful, confetti and silly string that he sprayed around that dark room, as if it might exorcise Peter's story. He listed the toys that he had brought to our house—D.C. and Marvel superheroes, Eagle Eye G.I. Joe, Star Wars characters, and the Death Star—and he suggested again that we turn on a light and play.

Peter shrugged. "Okay," he said. "If you want to see a werewolf."

"There's not a full moon," Jody said.

"You just can't see it because of the storm," Peter said.

"Let's get your toys," I said to Jody. "We can play with the light off."

The log had burned almost completely out, and the dim flame reflected in Peter's eyes. "Babies," he said. "Go ahead. Play with your little toys."

The toys were around the corner by the front door, and as Jody and I stepped onto the enclosed porch, he slipped his hand into mine. We grabbed the backpack and duffle bag that held the toys, and we hurried back around the corner, the windows following us like eyes.

Jody turned the backpack upside down in front of the fireplace, and toys spilled onto the carpet. I opened the Death Star, and Jody kneeled beside me. He dropped Princess Leia and Han Solo into the trash compactor and twisted the handle. The walls of the compactor slid together and squeezed the two figures out a hatch and onto the shag carpet. They lay side by side on their backs, their plastic hands touching. Jody scooped them up and handed them to me, and I dropped them into the compactor and twisted the handle.

While we played, Peter unzipped the duffle bag and pulled from it a plastic rifle with a parabolic dish at the end of the barrel. Jody told us it was a microphone. "You could hear people whisper from across the room," he said. He held up a pair of stethoscope-style earphones that dangled from the stock. "You put these in your ears, and point at what you want to hear."

Peter tried it first. I went across the room and whispered, "Mary had a little lamb." Peter repeated it.

"Go around the corner," he said, and I stepped around the corner, onto the porch.

"Whose fleece was white as snow," I whispered.

"White as snow," Peter said. "Cool." He pointed it through the kitchen toward our father's bedroom door, and for half a minute he sat listening. Then a smile worked across his face. He lowered the rifle and pulled the stethoscope tips from his ears. "Listen," he said, and he handed me the gun.

I put on the stethoscope and pointed the microphone at the bedroom door. Peter wasn't looking at me, but at Jody, still with that smile on his face, a smile like a finger drawn across a throat. The first sound I heard was Marcie's voice, a quiet moan. Then I heard my father. I couldn't make out his words, but he sounded as if he were giving instructions, the same tone of voice he had used on me the day we built Marcie's shed, the step-by-step commands as he walked me through my part. I heard Marcie's voice, a question, asking for clarification, and then my father's again, this time a snippet of clear words "Oh, for god's sake, not like that. Let me get it tight first." I heard another woman's voice, then, "Oh, Mr. Hardwick!" the tinny voice coming from the television on my father's dresser. Marcie moaned again, and then a man's voice from the TV moaned, and then Marcie, and then the other woman on the TV, and then my father. Then they were all moaning, a rhythmic chorus, call and answer, the sloshing of the waterbed marking time.

"Give the gun to Jody," Peter said.

I lowered the rifle and pulled the stethoscope ends from my ears. Jody was on his knees, still playing with Han Solo and Princess Leia. He had them facing each other, and he was wiggling one, and then the other, back and forth, as if they were carrying on a conversation. He didn't supply the words, and I had the feeling that he wasn't even thinking of words.

"Give Jody the gun," Peter said.

Jody didn't look up. I watched him wiggle those little people, watched them carry on some conversation that Jody was content to let go over his head, that was comfort enough just in the fact that it was happening at all.

"We should put another log on the fire," I said. The log had not burned completely, but had finally sputtered out, and now there was no flame, just a trickle of smoke and patchy red coals shimmering over the log's surface.

"Just give it to him first," Peter said.

"It's going to burn out," I said.

"So what? Give him the gun."

"Just leave him alone," I said, looking into the dark wood stove.

"You're his protector now?" Peter asked.

"No," I said.

I took the poker and prodded the log. A few orange sparks drifted up the chimney.

I could feel Peter behind me, staring at Jody, and then at me. "You're just going to screw it up," he said, as he picked the birch log up from the bricks. "Pull that log forward, and I'll drop this one behind."

I hooked the smoldering log with the poker and pulled it to the lip of the stove. Peter dropped the birch, too far forward, and it landed on the tip of the poker. The smoldering log slipped free and rolled out of the fireplace. It bounced with a shower of sparks off the brick base and landed on the living room carpet. We all jumped away as black smoke rose, the plastic fibers of the new shag melting beneath the charred wood. Peter grabbed the poker from my hand and pulled the ash shovel from its bucket. He pinched the log between the poker and shovel, but as he lifted, the log twisted out and melted another line of carpet. He tried again, and more of the carpet bubbled and threw up black smoke. Then the fire alarm rang out.

Peter was standing on the back of the couch, pulling the battery from the alarm when the bedroom door burst open, and our father ran naked into the living room. The curled bark of the paper birch caught fire and flared, spotlighting my father's body, his coat of hair glittering in the firelight. He stepped on a spot of melted carpet, and I heard a quick sizzle of flesh before he tossed back his head and howled. Jody backed against the wall. My father stepped again on the molten carpet and howled again. Jody still held his Star Wars figures, one gripped tightly in each fist. He was shaking, and though he seemed mentally to be somewhere else, I saw that his eyes were fixed on my father's penis, which jostled wildly as my father danced around the room on his burned feet.

I stared along with Jody, and for a moment there seemed nothing in that room but my father's penis. It banged back and forth off his inner thighs, always one beat behind as he went first for the log, and then for the fire poker, and then to the kitchen for a towel, and finally for the welcome mat on the front porch.

As he scooped the log up in the mat, I looked toward his open bedroom door. I could see one corner of his bed, and, on it, I saw Marcie's foot, a leather strap wrapped around her ankle. I looked again at Jody and saw that his expression of shock had settled into something more complex, something helpless and quietly desperate, the first expression I had seen on his face that didn't look as if it had been sculpted by a doll maker. And I saw that he was no longer looking at my father, but at the open bedroom door where, just out of his sight, his mother lay beneath the mirrors, wrists and ankles tied with leather straps, spread-eagle on that slick red satin sheet. Before I could stop him, Jody ran toward that open door.

We finished the shed just before sunset. Jody and Marcie had come out to see the final step, the hanging of the sliding doors, and they stood with me as Peter and my father fit the doors into their tracks. My father pulled them aside, and they stuttered hesitantly open. He slid them shut, and he and Peter joined us, his hand gripping the back of Peter's neck. "Thanks for the help, Son," he said.

The ground wasn't quite level, and the doors were out of square, an uneven gap between them. A dozen black spots showed on one side of the shed, where my father had used drywall screws to reattach the panel that he had fallen against. "It looks wonderful," Marcie said. My father nodded. An autumn breeze blew through the backyard, fluttering the corrugated vinyl panels, lifting the bottoms of the sliding doors away from the shed, and dropping them gently back against it.

"Well," my father said. "At least it'll never rust."

I never saw that shed again. I imagine it today, standing exactly as it had that autumn, whatever may have become of Jody and Marcie, whom I last saw on the morning following the storm, Marcie carrying Jody to her Toyota after the snowplow came through. I imagine the shed, unchanged, as winters pass and other women appear briefly in our lives. Unchanged, as the hair on my father's body turns silver, as his back curves into a buffalo hump. Unchanged, as he quietly drains the waterbed, takes the mirrors down from the ceiling, the wind on that bluff finally extinguishing the dim red ember of his remodeled bedroom. Unchanged, just like those Star Wars figures—us, not them, inevitably sliding into the long ago and the far away.

I held Han and Leia on that early June day at the yard sale as my wife stood framed by the garage door, pulling coins from her purse to pay for the picture books that our girls gripped tightly against their bodies. When she turned toward me, I held up Han and Leia and made them kiss. She smiled, a little sadly, and as our girls raced over with outstretched hands, she pulled out the billfold that she'd just put away. The Star Wars figures disappeared into the girls' fists, and I thought once more of Jody, of his face as he looked at the open bedroom door, and I realized that I had seen in his eyes the plight of us all, desperate to find a home as bright and lasting as that fantastic plastic.

THE BEGINNING OF LOSS

When Conrad read the letter from United Family Insurance, he saw that the matter was simple, a change of policy regarding loss and theft. He need only sign and return the enclosed form. He laid the papers on the dining-room table and took a pen from his shirt pocket, but as he was about to sign he saw that the insurance company required two signatures—policy holder and spouse. When, he wondered, as he set the pen down on the paper, had he last seen Susan?

He imagined himself walking through their living room as Susan lay curled on the couch reading a novel, something for her work on Slavic literature, a Czech or Polish surname—laced with czs and ies—stretching spine to fringe across the novel's cover. She would have glanced up from her book, told him there's tea on the stove.

Or maybe it hadn't been like that at all. Maybe she had just pulled aside the shower curtain, beads of water on her goose-bumped skin. Conrad would have been brushing his teeth, watching through the mirror as she reached for a towel, her feet still in the tub, her breast swaying with the extension of her arm.

Or maybe they'd passed in the windowless hallway upstairs, she carrying a basket of dirty clothes, he, a stack of student papers. It would have been a silent meeting, both of them pulled inward, tentative in the aftermath of a barely spoken argument.

But most likely, he thought, there wouldn't even have been the intimacy of bruised feelings. She would have been on the treadmill. He would have passed the open door, the flick of their eyes landing on each other for no greater space of time than a single footfall on the rolling tread.

But when did it start, Conrad wondered, as he stood in the dining room, the light of the setting sun washing golden over the insurance papers. What was the beginning of this loss?

There had been the day he couldn't find Susan as she did laundry. He had been sitting in the living room, grading a stack of essays about the origins of the Civil War, when he heard the lid to the washing machine swing open, the hollow bang of sheet metal drifting up the basement stairwell. He heard the rasp of the setting dial, the clack of engagement, the rush of water into the galvanized tub of clothes. The lid fell back into place, and he went back to his work.

He had just begun grading his fifth paper when the washer spun down. The buzzer sounded, and he realized that he hadn't seen Susan come up from the basement, though the door to the basement stairwell opened into the kitchen, in direct view of where he sat. He put down his papers, descended the stairs and found the laundry room empty.

The bare fluorescent bulb above the washer and dryer flickered, its ballast bad. The light blinked out, reignited, wavered. He tapped the glass tube and it brightened. Then it went out again, and for two seconds he was in complete darkness.

Just as the light flicked back to its half-life—waves traveling up and down the frosted glass—he heard water wash down the drainpipe behind him, the hum of more water in the copper pipe above his head. A toilet flushing.

He walked up to the main floor and checked the half-bath off the kitchen, but Susan wasn't there.

Theirs was an old Victorian home with two staircases from the main to the second floor—a front staircase with oak risers and a balustrade, and a narrow, servant's stairwell in the back. He walked up these back steps to the upstairs bathroom and found that it too was empty. He touched the faucet—still warm.

He was walking to the master bedroom, when he heard through a heat register the thunk of the washer lid and, a moment later, the rumble of the dryer. He went down the front staircase, and when he didn't pass Susan, he called down the basement stairwell. Nothing. He called again.

"I'm up here," she called down from the second floor.

He found her in their bedroom. She wore a running shirt and was pulling on fitted, polypropylene tights. They were just above her knees, and he watched the shrinking space of nakedness between the hem of her shirt and the rising band of the tights. She pulled them high, the polypropylene molding between her legs as the band snapped against her stomach.

"How did you get past me?" he asked.

"How did I get past you where?" she asked him.

"I don't know where."

"Well then I don't know how. I just switched the laundry."

"But earlier. I was in the living room, grading."

"I know."

"Did you see me?"

"I don't know," she said. "You're always in the living room grading." She stepped around him. "I'm running outside."

She was halfway down the hall when she turned back to him. "You could come, too," she said.

The doors to the rooms around her were closed, the hallway so dark that Conrad couldn't see her eyes. He saw, however, that she walked backward as she spoke. "No," he said. "You go ahead. I'm not dressed for it."

He listened to her trot down the stairs, heard the front door open, felt through the floor the weight of the oak and leaded glass as she pulled the door shut. I should have gone, he thought. I should go. But by the time he ran down the front stairs and onto the porch, the street was empty.

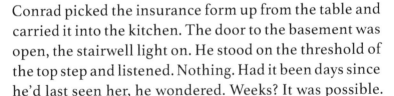

Conrad picked the insurance form up from the table and carried it into the kitchen. The door to the basement was open, the stairwell light on. He stood on the threshold of the top step and listened. Nothing. Had it been days since he'd last seen her, he wondered. Weeks? It was possible. But hadn't his loss begun long ago? Hadn't there been so very much loss before he'd ever met Susan?

There had been his parakeet who died under his mother's care when he'd been at his father's house for the summer. There had been the dogs—a collie, shot by the neighbor as it chased his sheep; a golden retriever, clumsy and slavish, sucked under the rear wheel of the school bus as it ran alongside Conrad's window, tongue out, wet brown eyes lolling up at him; and the two beagles who ran away together. He imagined the beagles running even now, leaping through the fallow

VINCENT REUSCH

fields that patched together the countryside around his father's house.

He took the insurance form with him, up the back stairwell to the bedroom. The bed had been made, and he tried to remember if he'd made it that morning before he left for school. Through the window, he saw a man and woman jogging along the sidewalk. They were younger than he and Susan, but not by much. Mid-thirties? The man said something, looked at the sky, spread his arms. The woman laughed and smacked his shoulder with her open hand. Conrad pulled his own shoulders back, tightened the muscles of his abdomen.

The day he lost Susan in the laundry room hadn't been the first time he'd lost her, he realized, as he looked from the runners to the sharp tuck of spread beneath the pillows. Earlier, there had been her disappearance from their bed.

Susan had been having problems sleeping and one day brought home blackout shades and a white-noise generator. She was up in her study when Conrad went to bed that night, and when something woke him he wasn't sure, in the darkness of the blackout shades, if it were still night or the next day. He thought at first that he was alone in the room, but then a ripple ran through the mattress and he knew that Susan was beside him. He thought that she was awake, and he wondered if her slipping in beside him was what had awoken him. She rolled from her back to her stomach, or from her stomach to her back. Or was it side to side? In the complete darkness and with the sound muted by the airy howl of the white-noise generator, he couldn't be sure.

Then Susan sighed. Or did she? He was sure she had, but then he doubted. Then he wondered if he'd introduced this doubt. If, in fact, he'd clearly heard her sigh, had clearly heard the loneliness and longing in that sigh. She shifted her body again, and Conrad shifted his, rolling to face whatever of her faced him, thinking that he should reach out. No matter the landing pad for his hand, it would be okay. He would be content with it. She would accept. But then he thought that she could as easily reach out to him. And he became stuck on this thought. And after a while of living in this consternated present, he heard above the hum of the noise maker the slow rhythm of his wife's somnolent breath.

For a long time, he lay awake, thinking alternately that she would still accept him if he reached for her, despite her sleep, and that she would roll away, despondent or even irritable at having been awoken.

The next morning, as he dressed in the darkness of the blackout shades, he used his cell phone as a flashlight, struggling to distinguish, in its dim electric glow, the colors of his shirts and ties. He shimmied into his pants, clasped the buckle of his belt in his hand so that it wouldn't make a noise. Then he tiptoed in his socks to the door and gently turned the knob.

But he paused as he slipped from the room, still haunted by his paralysis of the night before, as if the moment hadn't passed and he could still turn to Susan and let his hand fall where it may. He thought maybe he would kiss her cheek. He thought that this may make all the difference. But when the sliver of dawn light entered through the door and fell across the bed, Susan was not in it.

Conrad watched the runners stride off the sidewalk and across the grass of Rotary Park. The sun had dipped into the tops of the trees, and the light in the house had deepened to a honeyed glow. He thought that if he left the room and came back, Susan might appear in the bed. She might be napping. Or perhaps waiting for him, her body ready to acquiesce to his touch. He imagined himself undressing as she watched, imagined how shy he would feel standing naked in the autumn-chilled room with her smiling up at him, the sheet draped across the nape of her neck. He thought about the first time he'd seen her naked. It had been at night. She had been standing by a window, her pale body flattened in the dim but stark light of a streetlamp. Then he thought of the first time he'd seen any woman naked—a picture in a magazine—and he realized that there had been loss there too.

The magazine had been *Cheri*. Or had it been *Oui*? It might even have been *Juggs*, though when he thought of himself as a child opening the pages of *Juggs*, he wanted to reach into that past and fold the magazine closed, guide himself outside to play catch or frisbee, take himself to the museum of natural science, to the planetarium where he would lie beside his childhood self on reclining seats, and together they would watch the origins of the universe unfold above their heads.

He couldn't remember the name of the magazine because he'd had it for such a short time, its disappearance coming only hours after he'd stolen it from the top shelf of the closet in his father's bedroom. He was eleven, his parents two years divorced. He stashed the magazine in the garage, beneath a sagging cardboard box filled with old oil cans. He was sure, judging by the layers of dust on the rust-blistered cans, that the box hadn't been touched in years. But when he returned later that afternoon, he found the magazine missing.

What disturbed him most wasn't the loss of the magazine, however, but the implications of its near-immediate discovery, and the utter silence that followed.

First, there was the implication of knowledge. Someone—his father or his older brother—was far more aware of his movements than he'd realized. He had been sure he was unseen when he sneaked off to the garage with the magazine tucked into his pants, its glossy cover sticking to his sweating stomach. But both his brother and his father had been home, his father sorting through jars of nuts and bolts in the basement, his brother upstairs in his bedroom. Either could have heard him slip into his father's closet, he supposed, the creak of the old farmhouse's wooden floor, the click of the door latch. Either could have seen him cross the lawn to the garage—his brother from behind his blue curtains, his father through the sideways rectangle of the basement window. But even if they had seen him, who would have thought anything of it? Who would have waited until he'd left his hiding place, and then gone in after him to rummage through the cluttered garage and retrieve the magazine?

Then, after several days of no repercussion, there was the implication of motive, for with no reprisal, the motive evidently wasn't to expose his theft or depravity. Either his brother wanted the magazine, or his father wanted the magazine back. Because Conrad didn't know which, he could only imagine both, and he felt surrounded by the knowledge. Somehow, when he'd come across the stack of magazines weeks earlier in his father's closet, he hadn't followed the logic of his discovery. He had thought of manhood and sex. He hadn't thought of his father, alone at night in bed with the magazines. Now he was plagued by this thought. And when this image wasn't in his mind, it was replaced by the same scene with his brother in the lead role. For several months, he wished he'd never found the magazines. But he thought of them. Often.

The second magazine he stole was *Club*. This time, he waited until his father and brother were away from home.

He had thought this second trip to his father's closet would reveal the identity of his watcher. Either his father had reclaimed the magazine, or it would still be missing, leaving no doubt about his brother. Conrad had, in fact, told himself—ignoring the aching heat in his belly—that the solution to this mystery was the reason for this second foray into his father's closet. But when he pulled the stack down from the shelf, he saw that the magazines were different from those he had found the first time. As he sifted through this new stack, he wondered, with a tinge of pain, where the others had gone, all those women who had offered so much of themselves.

He still remembered the woman on the cover of the *Club* that he slid from this new stack. Her blue gym shorts and tiny white shirt. Her feathered, sun-touched hair. Her glossy lips, parted just enough to reveal a slight gap between her front teeth.

He had been captivated by this gap, which felt more intimate than anything he saw of this woman inside the magazine. It felt like an opening into her life, and through it he could hear the sound of her voice. He could smell her, the scent of a vanilla candle. Could see her snacking on popcorn in the blue glow of the TV on a Saturday night.

He imagined this gap in her school pictures, unchanging through the years, as her hairstyles progressed, as her eyes reflected new understandings—this stubbornly constant space that spoke of her whole life. He could see her, five years old in pajamas, tearing open a present on Christmas morning. He could see her among the eighth-grade girls, just out of his reach, willing to play four-square with him at lunch recess, but not returning his wave as she stood with the other eighth-graders on the sidewalk outside the QuickMart. And he could see her at his own age, sneaking glances at him from two desks over, as Mrs. Winston diagrammed sentences on the blackboard. Conrad's fingers felt thick as he opened the magazine, and he worked his way through it slowly, peeling away her layers page by glossy page.

He hid the *Club* on top of a length of heating duct that ran along the ceiling of the basement, reached with a step ladder that hung from the wall nearby. Because he'd hidden this magazine inside the house, and because he felt so vulnerable to detection using the ladder, he rarely saw the photographs of this woman. But when, several months later, the magazine disappeared, he found that though he hardly remembered the details of her body, he could perfectly imagine her presence in his life. At times, he knew, she would be completely inaccessible, her eyes distant, something in them of the glossy magazine. But these times he could endure if it meant that she would eat popcorn with him on a Saturday night, that she would lie in his bed, would stay up all night with him and listen to how he felt about Jenny in his social studies class, let him put his tongue between her glossy lips and touch that space between her teeth.

VINCENT REUSCH

He couldn't remember when this woman from the cover of the *Club* magazine ceased to appear, when he last conjured her viscerally in his mind. He realized only now, after so many years, that she was lost to him, reduced to the photograph on the magazine's cover. As he realized this loss, he felt guilty, as if in his neglect he had done her some harm, as if she were somewhere waiting for him. In a small gray room, he imagined, sitting on the edge of a worn mattress.

There had been the tea, Conrad thought. He was in Susan's study now. An afghan lay across the sofa. The treadmill was folded up, the tread raised and locked. The put-away feeling of the treadmill struck Conrad hotly. Susan rarely folded it up, and there was a feeling of permanence about it. A few raisins huddled in the bottom of a dish on her desk. But who could tell with raisins? They might have been there for months.

Before the incident with the washer and dryer, before the empty bed, with the sheets pushed aside like that and the impression of Susan's head still on the pillow, there had been the appearance of the tea, an appearance that had marked another disappearance. Conrad had been reading in the living room, Susan running on the treadmill in her study above him. The tea was still hot, steam curling from the lip of the cup, the tea's surface alive with concentric rings that rose in time with the rhythm of the treadmill.

"Where did this come from?" Conrad asked Susan, as she passed through the living room after her run.

"It's tea," she said.

"I know it's tea," he said. "But how did it get here?"

"I brought it to you."

"But you were running. And I didn't hear the kettle."

"I made us tea, Con. It's not a mystery."

She knew that he had been reading a mystery. Agatha Christie. He had read so many that he couldn't keep track of them, realizing often only at the moment of reveal that he had read that book before.

When the tea appeared a second time, Susan was weeding the flower beds in front of the house. "I'm telling you," Conrad said, "you weren't here."

"I'm taking a bath," Susan said.

He couldn't remember when the last cup had appeared, but they had continued for weeks. Or was it months? Sometimes the tea was still hot, and he drank it. Other times it was hours old, the essence of flowers now an oily veneer on the tea's cool surface.

As he left Susan's study, Conrad remembered another waiting. Another loss. Captain Bunny Bunny, when he was five years old.

He had realized that Captain Bunny Bunny was gone after his mother had tucked him into bed. As her hip weighted down the mattress, the *Big Book of Grimm* settling onto her lap, he reached for Captain Bunny Bunny but found only an empty space where the bed met the wall.

At first, he refused to believe that his bunny could be missing. It was simply too much to grasp. He couldn't remember a time before Captain Bunny Bunny.

The bunny was large, half as tall as Conrad, and Conrad had carried it everywhere with him, dragging it along the linoleum tile of the kitchen, pulling it through the yard in his Radio Flyer wagon, sitting on the floor with it to watch Saturday morning cartoons, three feet from the television screen. When he was excited, he gripped the bunny as hard as he could and held on until he felt the wave of energy subside, and when he was anxious, he sucked on the tips of its ears.

Over time, Captain Bunny Bunny's stuffing had broken down into a dozen or so clumps the size of balled fists, and Conrad liked to hold one in his hand as he fell asleep.

When he didn't feel Captain Bunny Bunny where it was supposed to be, in bed with him listening to the Brothers Grimm, he threw back his blanket. No Captain Bunny Bunny. His mother stood, and they looked together under the bed. No Captain Bunny Bunny. She went to search downstairs, and he waited beneath his covers, not daring to think of the possibility that she may return without his rabbit. When she stepped empty-handed back into the circle of lamplight by his bed, he began to shake.

Although he was hardly able to comprehend his loss, he was able to blame, and he blamed his mother. Viciously. After all, wasn't it obvious? She had been saying for weeks that Captain Bunny Bunny was getting old. Wouldn't he like to rest on a shelf, she'd ask. Wouldn't Conrad like to pick out a new bunny?

His anger at his mother manifested itself most visibly in public, as he sensed the greater damage it did within view of an audience. He screamed in grocery stores. He fell, dead weight, onto sidewalks. He held the edge of the car door as she tried to push him into the backseat.

Despondency followed his anger, and for weeks he thought of almost nothing at all. When he pushed his matchbox cars along the designs in the dining-room rug, he didn't think about who was in the cars or where they were going. And when he switched to his Tonka fire truck, he pushed it lazily, as if whatever school or house or hospital were burning might just as well burn.

When he tired of pushing his cars and trucks, he sat by the living-room window and watched his father rake maple leaves into piles in the front yard, the bright oranges and reds not tempting him to come outside, even when his father waved a gloved hand for Conrad to join him.

Then the new bunny arrived.

When he awoke in the morning to the new rabbit, Conrad squeezed it against himself. A rush of heat flooded his body, welling up like tears. He felt himself filled with love and relief and gratitude. Until he realized that something was terribly wrong. This rabbit was thick and springy, its stuffing made of a spun, plasticky fiber. It had a bitter scent that reminded him of the burdock patch beside the barn, a place where he and Captain Bunny Bunny liked to play, breaking the stalks aside and forming tunnels among the bushes' broad leaves. They had only recently been forced to abandon their burdock fort as the cockleburs had browned with the coming of autumn, and his mother had scolded him as she picked the burs from the laces of his shoes.

When Conrad put his mouth over the tips of this new rabbit's ears—suckling now on the very source of his anxiety—the taste, too, was like the bitter milk of those broken burdock stalks.

He threw the new rabbit from his bed, and all morning he cried hot, angry tears, his fingers remembering the feel of Captain Bunny Bunny's cotton fists, his mouth the taste of those stained ears and the sieve-like quality of the cloth when it had become soaked with his saliva. When he imagined Captain Bunny Bunny too vividly, he would writhe in pain and fall again to sobbing. But he couldn't help but imagine him, run his mind over him, an elephant running its trunk along the bones of its dead. Nothing in his short life had hurt as deeply as this act of remembrance, and nothing had ever seemed so necessary.

As fall gave way to winter, Conrad's depression eased, but even so, he rejected the new bunny until Valentine's Day, when his mother showed him the chocolate eggs that it had lain, and he finally gave it a name. Captain Rabbit.

The sun had set and the palette of the house had shifted from warm to cool. Conrad stood now in the bathroom, and the white porcelain of the fixtures around him glowed the pale blue of late-evening snow. He pulled back the shower curtain. Ridiculous, he knew.

He was leaving the bathroom when he saw on the floor, in the corner by the sink, a single earring, and he thought maybe he remembered. The beginning of their loss.

They had been eating dinner at Capelli's. Susan had ordered the eggplant parmesan. Conrad had ordered spaghetti with meatballs, recipe of the owner's grand-mother. Between them was a bottle of Chianti wrapped in straw. The occasion was Susan's thirty-ninth birthday. She looked away as he filled her wine glass, and he saw that she was missing an earring. It was not expensive, a bohemian garnet he'd bought for her on the street during a trip to Poland.

They had taken the trip just before they'd married, paid for by her research grant. They had visited the childhood home of Czesław Miłosz, had attended a reading by Marcin Świetlicki. Conrad hadn't understood Świetlicki's words, only his tone, which had sounded angry and bleak, and as Susan nodded and laughed dryly along with the small audience, Conrad felt himself somehow at the center of their disdain.

When he pointed out the missing earring at the restaurant, Susan pinched her earlobe between her thumb and finger. "Hmm," she said. "I'll have to look for it."

Maybe if they had met on their hands and knees right then under the table, things would have turned out differently. But they hadn't met under the table. They hadn't looked for the earring at all. They had hardly even looked at each other. The loss was already there, somewhere in the air between them.

Now, as he left the earring on the bathroom floor where it lay, Conrad thought that he would never find the beginning, would never know the end. He would never be able to count the days, add them up, name the cause. How could he, when even the loss of a five-year-old's stuffed rabbit could be so complicated—the pain of loss, the acceptance, and then the tragedy of the return.

It was spring when Conrad spotted Captain Bunny Bunny from across the yard. Snow still lay, icy and pocked, in the shadow of the barn and the hollows of the forest floor. Conrad wore a brown corduroy coat and red-white-

and-blue plaid pants, his newly named Captain Rabbit dangling from his hand.

Captain Bunny Bunny sat on a stump that had, by last summer's end, been overgrown with burdock. It was the stump that had been at the center of Conrad's burdock fort, hidden among the broad leaves. Now the remains of last year's burdock lay at the stump's feet, brown snaking stalks and decayed leaves, matted down from the weight of the winter's snow. From the distance of the house, the stuffed rabbit was little more than a pebble in the landscape of woods and barn, but Conrad recognized it at once, his eyes intimate with those contours that his mind had spent so many hours caressing in absentia.

He squeezed his new bunny's wrist as he walked toward Captain Bunny Bunny.

Halfway across the yard, he could see that one of the rabbit's ears had flopped over. He remembered the plastic strips that had held the ears erect, how he used to feel them in his mouth through the plush fabric, how when the fabric was wet enough he could feel with his tongue that one of the strips had raised bumps that might have been letters. As he stepped closer, he saw that the rabbit's color had changed, its once creamy belly now yellowed. Closer, and he saw that one of its eyes was missing, a tuft of white fluff poking through the hole where the eye had been. The other eye, a black bead, hung like a spider from its loosened thread.

As he stepped off the threshold of the yard and onto the tangle of last year's burdock, he saw that one of the arms had separated from the shoulder. Closer, and he saw that the rabbit's fur was covered in a disease of black specks—spores or mold or insect droppings.

He heard the screen door of the house spring open and slap shut. He grabbed a stick from the ground. His mother shouted from behind him. He looked at her, and she waved. She was wearing her straw gardening hat, and she held tools in her hand—a trowel and something with bent prongs that looked like the foot of an enormous bird. She seemed about to go on her way, but then one hand went to her hip, the other to her forehead as if to block the sun from her eyes, despite the hat's wide, floppy brim.

Conrad turned back to the rabbit and held the stick shaking in front of himself. He thought of the months that Captain Bunny Bunny had waited for his return. Thought how it must have been that first night, the woods growing dark around him. The hope he must have had when the sun rose the next day.

How many days had hope endured, Conrad would go on to wonder in the following days, weeks, and years. How often did it return, flicker, fade? There had been the fall rains, thunderstorms. But there had been the Indian summer, too, crisp sunny days that would have dried the rabbit's fur and warmed him to the core. The first snowfall must have been beautiful. Had he awoken to it covering the ground as Conrad had? Or had he watched the flakes drift down, silver against the black sky?

But what of these moments of peace? Wouldn't he have been better off without their prolonging the hope? How long had hope remained with no grounds? How many weeks of neglect equal one week too many? If Conrad had found his rabbit midwinter, would he have been able to salvage it, or had the fall rains already done too much damage?

His mother shouted his name from the yard behind him, her voice rising on the second syllable. "Conrad?" A centipede emerged from the rabbit's missing eye, ran down its cheek and across its narrow chest. Conrad thrust the stick forward, and Captain Bunny Bunny toppled off his stump.

"Susan!" Conrad called. He was once again in the dining room. Evening had ebbed toward night, and in the deep twilight the room looked as if it were veiled in dust, the insurance form for loss and theft ancient in his hand.

The quiet of the house felt different after he called to Susan. It felt thick, as if Susan had stopped what she was doing and was holding still. He felt this thick quiet around every corner, the house filled with Susans, all standing in perplexed silence just out of his sight. A stripe of yellow light fell from the open basement door and lay across the kitchen linoleum, and as Conrad walked toward it a hollow bang of metal sounded from the basement, the hinged lid of the washing machine. There was the rasp and clack of the control dial, the rush of water into the galvanized tub. Then there was a footstep on the basement stairs. Conrad stopped at the threshold to the kitchen. The staircase creaked under the weight of another footstep. Tired sounds, Conrad thought. Or angry. Or resigned. Or were they sad? The lamentation of the wooden risers. "Susan?" he said again. "Suze?"

A shadow interrupted the stripe of light on the kitchen floor. And as Conrad waited to see what would emerge, he thought of the first night that he and Susan had shared a bed. How he had cupped her breast in his hand as he fell asleep. And how good that felt. How warm. How wonderful when he woke in the night and found his hand still there, rising and falling with the motion of her breath.

THE YELLOW SCOOTER

Geenie and L.B. looked lovingly at the yellow scooter, and, pinched as it was in the middle of a phalanx of gray and black motorbikes, it seemed to smile back at them, a bright little cherub of a scooter, waiting to be adopted. The shopkeeper laid his bowl of *jjigae* on the floor and stood behind the young American couple. He put one arm around each of them and hissed the Korean word, *choda*. Good. Two of his teeth, capped in gold, gleamed as he swiveled his grin from Geenie to L.B. and back again, his face so close that they could smell in his breath the chili and garlic soup. Good price, he said in rough English.

It was true, the price was good, almost too good. Only for you, he said when L.B. asked why. Only today.

He poured two cups of green tea and motioned Geenie and L.B. to sit on plastic stools while he checked the tires and wiped down the scooter. He bolted a cable-lock to the rear rack and strapped on a bungee cord. Service, he said, which meant free. L.B. chose two matching yellow helmets. For safety, he said. We'll stand out from the crowd.

The shopkeeper's fingers whirred through the thick stack of ten-thousand-won bills that L.B. handed him.

Majayo, he said, and he wheeled the scooter onto the sidewalk and waited to bow, while L.B. and Geenie fussed with their helmets and propped themselves on their yellow prize.

Geenie smiled inside her big yellow helmet. Buckle your seat belt, smiley face, L.B. said. He pushed the starter button, and the engine bubbled to life. Hang on, he shouted.

Roger, Geenie shouted back, and L.B. coddled the scooter off the sidewalk and into the street. In his rearview mirror, a small cat's-eye oval, he saw the shopkeeper bow and smile, his teeth looking now as if they had been made of iron and had begun to rust. *Annyeonghi gaseyo*, the shopkeeper said. May you go in peace.

Buying the scooter had been Geenie's idea, but it couldn't have made L.B. happier. Her English-teaching contract would be finished in two months, and though she hadn't said she wouldn't sign again, she hadn't said she would, either. Adding to his concern, a week earlier he had seen the title of an email in her inbox while he stood behind her at an internet cafe. It was entitled "RE: Inquiry," and the return address was such-and-such at phs.edu. For a week he fretted about why she hadn't mentioned it, and whether he should, when, on a sweltering afternoon in Geenie's apartment, she started a conversation with the words, I've been thinking. Just as his world floated out from beneath L.B., she said, it might be fun if we had a scooter.

On the ride home, L.B. made sure to use his blinkers at every turn. He came to full stops, putting both feet down at each stop sign. When a car looked like it might turn out in front of him, he honked his horn, or, as Geenie liked to say, he beeped it. Beep at him, she'd shout from behind him. Beep at him!

On the way to L.B.'s apartment they stopped at Nambu Shijang, a large market by the river. They didn't often come to Nambu market, because the taxi fare was too expensive. Things will be different now, L.B. said. We can go wherever we want. He unwound the cable from the rack and threaded it through the rear wheel, delicately, as if he were changing a newborn's diaper.

They both glanced back as they walked away.

As they strolled beneath the canopy of colored umbrellas and tarps, Geenie pointed out this thing and that, tables and curtains and appliances. This would go great in your living room, she'd say, or, wouldn't it be nice to have that in the kitchen. L.B. took her hand as she spelled out her plans for turning his cramped two-room apartment into a home. The market *ajummas*, the farmer's wives, waved garlic and cabbage and ray fish in front of them. Geenie and L.B. said thank you and no thank you and it looks delicious and we're American and a few other of the handful of Korean phrases that took care of their daily lives. They bought a chicken and some garlic and vegetables and carried them back to the scooter. L.B. lifted the seat, and Geenie put the food in the small trunk that was hidden beneath. Then they drove from the market to a hardware store, where they bought a heavy chain and a padlock. The man gave us a lock, Geenie said as L.B. hefted the tails of spooled chain that dripped from the ceiling of the store.

It only locks around the wheel, he told her. A couple guys could just load it into a pickup truck and drive away.

To spare the tomatoes, Geenie held the chain in her lap as L.B. drove them to his apartment. They squeezed out of the forest of high-rises and looped around a spiral drive to his apartment, a four-story walkup that sat removed on a small hill. He eased the scooter in beside a bicycle rack, cut the engine, and padlocked the chain around a steel tube on the side of the rack. Then he locked the scooter's cable to the chain. There, he told her. We'll lock it like that.

They made a chicken stir-fry dinner that evening. Geenie put some music on the stereo, and they danced as they cooked, bumping hips and spinning each other around the tiny kitchen. I don't think I've ever seen you dance, Geenie said.

When they made love that night, it was light and frolicking and entirely different from their recent love-making, which had been quick and well rehearsed, ending often with Geenie rolling onto her side and L.B. lying on his back, looking at the ceiling. They made love that night on the living room floor beside their dinner dishes, and, for a brief time, on the porch. I want to see our car, Geenie said in the middle of their romance, and they stumbled together to the railing with as little interruption as possible. It's glowing, she said looking down. I think we brought it to life.

For the next few weeks Geenie stayed with L.B., going home only for clothes and necessities. L.B. insisted on going with her when he could. Those kids on your corner, he told her, they're always watching us come and go. Geenie said they were good kids, but it was true that she lived in a rough area, and she knew of three scooters that had been stolen from her parking lot that year. Each time he and Geenie drove out of her apartment complex, L.B. glared at the Korean teenagers, their white shirts untucked beneath their school blazers. They usually ignored him, but sometimes one would say something that L.B. didn't understand, and the others would laugh. They're trouble, L.B. would say. They're just boys, Geenie would say.

———

Now that they had the scooter, they abandoned the local restaurants and grocery stores near L.B.'s apartment, and, instead, drove to Nambu market. The fish is so much fresher there, L.B. would say—or the chicken, or the spinach, or the mushrooms. Not to mention cheaper, Geenie would add.

When they didn't need food, they thought of other things they needed. They never sat down and made lists as they had when they rode buses and taxis. We're out of dish soap, Geenie would declare, and they'd grab their helmets and bolt out the door. When they needed a light bulb they drove to a specialty lighting shop across town, and when their knives grew dull from all the cooking they'd been doing, Geenie said, I saw this cutlery place over in Samcheon-dong. And every time they came home, L.B. carefully locked the scooter to the bike rack.

One Saturday, Geenie suggested that they get out of the city. They packed two lunches in the trunk and wound down L.B.'s drive into the shade of the surrounding buildings, where they threaded their way through the landscape of Korean traffic and into the countryside.

The country roads were narrow and winding, perched half a dozen feet above the rice paddies, with no shoulder or guardrail. L.B. drove lazily under the warm sunshine and, as he veered wide on a turn, Geenie peeked over the edge of the pavement. Watch where you're going, she shouted, and she held on tighter.

Houses with bowed roofs topped in heavy curled tiles slid by, and apple and pear orchards fanned out across the slopes that rose from the paddies. Men in green or yellow waders dotted the lowlands, and an occasional *halmeoni*, grandmother, toddled down the road, bent in two and leaning on a cane. L.B. drove and Geenie talked and sometimes he heard her and sometimes not, and they buzzed through the countryside, leaving a faintly sweet-smelling blue haze in their wake.

After their picnic and an ambling drive back to town—with the top down, as Geenie said—they parked by the river at Nambu market and walked along the shore, watching the old men fish and gamble beneath the bridge. The men, growing used to seeing Geenie and L.B., tore off strips of dried squid for the young couple to chew on, and on cool evenings, they would pass L.B. a small glass of *soju* to warm his belly. The market *ajummas* pulled Geenie now and again up the slope, and she squatted in their circle, picking at some root or vegetable with them while they chatted and stroked her arms with fingers that were mostly knuckle.

At first, Geenie and L.B. cooked mostly stir-fries and seafood and some Korean soups, *jjigaes*, but as their cooking continued, their meals became increasingly western—meat and potatoes, bread and pasta, with red wines to wash it down. Geenie composed a song that she sang when they made chicken and potatoes. She called it Bangers and Mash—despite L.B.'s correction that the meal wasn't technically bangers and mash—and she drummed out the rhythm with chicken legs on the counter. Together they'd polish off the whole chicken, a small cauldron of mashed potatoes, corn, kimchi, and, always now, dessert.

Our clothes are shrinking, Geenie complained one morning while L.B. lay on his back, trying to fasten the button on his jeans.

That's one way to look at it, he said.

The altercation with the driver of the black sedan happened on their way home from Nambu market. They had a chrome toaster-oven bungeed to the back of the scooter. Cookies, Geenie had said when they'd found it. Cake. And, dreamily, pie.

Given L.B.'s recent driving habits, it wasn't surprising that a problem would arise. He no longer put both feet down at stop signs, and his philosophy of turn signals had changed from using them as a cautionary device to using them as a warning. Ready or not, the blinking lights said, here I come. When he came to a red light, rather than stay in his place in line, he now popped onto the sidewalk and drove up to the intersection, and then dropped back into the road ahead of the cars. Soon, from watching other scooters and motorbikes, he learned the trick of swerving close to the oncoming traffic lane and riding along the double yellow lines to the front of the pack.

You shouldn't do that, Geenie would say, but then she'd squeeze him and nuzzle the visor of her helmet into his shoulder. He'd reach back and pinch her on the butt, honking the horn in time with his pinches. Beep beep, the horn would sound. Beep beep, Geenie would say, and they'd buzz away at the green light, leaving the throng of traffic behind them.

The black sedan's right turn signal was blinking. It was stopped at a light with several cars in front of it, and L.B. had just begun to ease by, squeezing between the car's right side and the curb. There were only a couple feet of space, and, with Geenie and the toaster oven on the back, he was driving slowly. Just as he drew up parallel with the rear tire, the car crept over and cut off his path. Son of a bitch, L.B. yelled, and he beat with his fist on the tinted rear-side window.

The man who slid from the driver's door wore a black tailored suit. His hair was spiked and shiny. *Ggampae*, Geenie whispered. Gangster. He was thick and stubby, but he moved around his car with such a graceful precision that L.B. became mesmerized, not taking his eyes off the driver, almost as if for fear the man would drop to all fours and lunge for L.B.'s throat. And for his part, the driver didn't take his eyes off L.B. And such eyes they were, narrow and yellowed, two unlit matchsticks.

L.B. took off his helmet, flicked down the kickstand and stood between the man and Geenie. *Mwoya*, he said. What the hell. He waved his arm at the sealed path between the car and the curb. The man brought his wide face near the right rear window where L.B. had hit the car. He put his forearm to the spot and slowly buffed out the prints. Then he straightened himself and turned his flat yellow eyes toward L.B. and Geenie and the scooter.

Listen, L.B. said uneasily, I don't care who you are.

The gangster looked up and down the road in the same slow way he had looked at L.B.'s handprints.

I don't care what kind of car you drive, L.B. said.

The man walked back around his car and opened his door.

I have a right to a life, too, damn it.

The man looked one last time at L.B. Then he sealed himself back into his car, behind his tinted windows, and L.B. got back on the scooter. Geenie wrapped her arms around him.

Wow, that was great, baby, she said. You're my knight in shining armor. She hugged him tightly as she described the scene back to him, play-by-play, her heart beating against his back. As he listened, L.B. weighed her current positive response against the email he'd seen the day before in her inbox.

The latest email was titled "Invitation" and again was from such-and-so at phs.edu, undoubtedly a high school teaching offer. He saw this one while she was checking her email at his apartment, and somehow it hurt worse seeing it there. The new mint curtains they'd bought seemed suddenly heavy and darker than they'd looked in the market. The ink painting, bamboo in the wind, that they had been so proud to have found tucked in the back of a quiet gallery, now looked sinister, the trees like skeletal fingers reaching toward him. Even their new *ibul*, the quilt on their bed, had gathered up around his neck the night he saw the email, and he'd woken up dreaming he was suffocating.

Another week passed, the third since they'd bought the scooter, and they continued shopping. They bought an ironing board, a set of pots and pans, matching striped pajamas—powder blue for him, pink for her—a low floor-seating table and two cushions. Geenie fussed over their new things, studying the few remaining empty corners and blank spaces of walls, mumbling lists of possible additions, while L.B. whipped up delicacies in the kitchen. He experimented with sauces and roux. He blanched and sautéed and puréed, and one time Geenie told him she thought he might have even fricasseed. He told her he'd fricassee her, and she said he'd *rue* the day. And in this way they bantered and pinched and squeezed and chewed their way through their evenings.

After dinner and dessert, while the dishes waited piled in the sink, and the crimson wine meditated in pools in the bottoms of their cups, they lounged together, pajama-clad, in their comfortably crowded apartment. Only slowly would they emerge, as if they'd just spent a night sleeping lightly in each other's arms. Geenie would say beep beep or L.B. would say fricassee, and their soft play would turn into lovemaking, the flannel pajamas a pleasing barrier. They made love on the floor beside their new table. They made love in the bathtub and on the sink. They made love on the porch and in front of the open refrigerator door. That was Geenie's favorite place. I want a grape, she would say. Or an apple, or a piece of pie, and they'd work their way, conjoined, to the refrigerator.

Geenie was a fast typist, and the clacking sound of the keys as she wrote her emails had chased L.B. from his apartment. I'm going to get a checkup on the scooter, he'd said, and she'd said, mm-hmm, without looking up from the screen.

He drove up and down the street, trying to remember exactly where the shop had been. Like most Korean streets, the walks were lined with small stores of every kind, all piled on top of each other and packaged in bright colors and neon signs. People and cars and bicycles jockeyed for position on the street and sidewalk, and L.B. worked his way through the tangle while scanning the signs for the scooter shop. He bumped a woman with his handlebar, and she scolded him, tipping her head back to indicate the baby who rode in the pocket of a quilt slung over her shoulder. A car locked its brakes as L.B. veered into the wrong lane while looking at what turned out to be a row of bicycles. He tried the streets on either side of the one he was on, knowing that they weren't the correct streets, and after several slow passes and a few more close calls with cars and pedestrians, he gave up. The skin on his forehead prickled as sweat broke out beneath his helmet.

He had just gotten back up to speed when he saw the sedan in his mirror. It was just a flick of black between two cars as it changed lanes far behind him, but L.B. had no doubt that it was the gangster. Even its windshield was tinted black, he noticed, when it had drawn close enough, or crept up he might say, for it certainly seemed that way. He turned right, and it turned right. He turned again, and it followed. And each time he looked into his cat's-eye mirror, it was closer than before.

He found his opportunity for escape at a red light with the sedan just a few car-lengths behind. It was long and low in his mirror now, and he could hear the deep growl of its engine. He swerved left, darted up the double yellow lines to the front of the pack, then turned right, cutting across three lanes of cars that had just begun to move as the light changed to green. The bumper of the farthest car missed his rear tire by a foot. He gave the scooter all the gas he could. The engine whined, and the scooter slowly built up speed and carried him safely into the clearing that surrounded his apartment. He locked the scooter to the bike rack and waited for his pulse to slow.

Chocolate chip, Geenie said when he walked into the apartment, and she held a spoonful of dough up to his mouth. What happened to you, she asked. You're sweating.

Nothing, he said. I just had a thing on the scooter.

A thing? Are you okay?

Yeah, just some jackass driver.

Did he cut you off?

Something like that. It's okay, really.

What did the scooter-man say?

He wasn't there. The shop's gone.

Gone?

You know how it is here, he said.

You know that cutlery place is out of business, too, she said. You can't count on anything here. Enjoy it while it lasts.

L.B. saw the car often after that, always far in the background like a spot of ink on his mirror, and no matter how he drove, he couldn't wipe it off. He veered suddenly onto sidewalks, dropped hard off curbs, bumped car mirrors as he snaked between lanes, and sent pedestrians stumbling into each other at crosswalks. At first Geenie didn't seem to mind the growing recklessness. She complained teasingly as she always had, but she also hugged him and nuzzled his shoulder as she always had. Beep beep, she said on an afternoon when he blew past a line of cars and ran a red light. When he didn't pinch her she said beep beep again. When he finally did pinch her, it was hard as he strained to see if the car was still in his mirror. Ouch, she complained. That's not the way it goes.

They had been driving home from the market when the accident happened. Their trunk was loaded with fruit, a small ham, and an ice cream cake. It's the scooter's birthday, Geenie had said. One month. We need a cake.

L.B. was sure he'd just seen the black car, and, lost in his mirror, he didn't realize that traffic had stopped until Geenie screamed. He pulled the brake levers, the scooter wobbled, and they tumbled to the pavement, the ham and the fruit spilling out of the trunk and rolling aimlessly on the road. Geenie sat on the pavement wide-eyed, pulling her hand from the cake, while L.B. and a helpful motorist picked up the scooter and some of the food. *Kamsahamnida*, L.B. said to the driver, and he straddled the scooter and motioned for Geenie to get on. For a moment she looked at him as if she didn't know him. Hurry, he said. The traffic.

After he locked the scooter, L.B. ran his hand along the scar that was gouged into the plastic panel on its side. The left blinker hung from its electrical wire, its stalk broken.

They made scalloped potatoes and ham for dinner. L.B. cubed the ham, and beside him Geenie sliced the potatoes. They didn't put on any music, and neither of them spoke other than those things they needed to say to coordinate their cooking. Where did you put the measuring spoons? How much milk do we need? I thought it was in the drawer. I don't know.

While their dinner cooked in the toaster oven, Geenie checked her email, and L.B. looked fretfully out the window. The side of the high-rise apartment building next door filled his view. Every apartment was lit, and he could see the chalky silhouettes of children moving behind curtains, and in almost every apartment the arrhythmic pulsing of a television set, most of them tuned to the same channel, so that the apartments blinked in time with each other, as if in a state of perfect communication.

After they ate dinner and dessert, Geenie turned the computer on again and quickly checked her email. L.B., she said, her voice low and serious.

I'm sorry, he said. I just wasn't looking where I was going.

No, baby, it's not that. It's just, she said. I just . . .

But whatever words she was searching for wouldn't come, or the strength to say them, or the desire. Their stomachs were full of ham and cookies, and the apartment was warm and comfortable, holding them in its domestic hug, arms fashioned from upholstery and flannel and lamplight and red wine.

We're being followed, L.B. said. He spoke quickly and a little too loudly as he told her about the car, and for a moment she looked at him as she had in the street while he was scrambling to pick up the fruit.

But there must be dozens of cars like that in the city, she said.

I know, he said. But the tinted windows.

A lot of those big cars have tinted windows.

But this one is stalking us.

I want to see it, she said.

It's there, baby.

I believe you. Just tell me next time you see it. She turned off the computer and sat in his lap.

Dinner was good, L.B. said. I think that pavement tenderized the ham.

I think it tenderized my ham, too, Geenie said.

I'll tenderize your ham, L.B. said. He lit a candle and clicked off the lamp.

What do you think he wants, Geenie asked. Do you think he saw us fall? Maybe he'll be satisfied with that.

They sat in the candlelight and Geenie speculated: Maybe they wanted to kidnap them and take them to their hideout. Maybe they'd torture them in some ritualistic Asian gang ceremony. Maybe they would chop up their bodies and bury the pieces in the mountains. Her voice became an excited whisper as she imagined increasingly grizzly and bizarre scenarios.

Do you think they'll tear off our fingernails, she asked.

They'll never catch us, he said.

They made love there in the candlelight, with her still in his lap, and they continued in front of the open refrigerator, where Geenie pulled and cajoled him. I can't stop thinking about that yogurt, she said.

Afterward, as they lay in the dark bedroom, she moved her head to his chest. The big bad wolf is after us, she said.

I guess that would make us two little piggies, L.B. said.

We're sure starting to look like piggies.

I guess we are, he said, and he brushed his fingers through her hair. I just hope we built our house strong enough.

Two days later, L.B. found the scooter unlocked. Geenie had taken it to her apartment the previous evening, saying she needed to get some clothes. While she was away L.B. logged onto the internet and stared numbly at the bright yellow smiley face next to Geenie's name in his online address book. Above it and below was a column of gray faces with sleeping eyes and mouths, each gray face followed by the name of a friend or family member. He had told himself he was only going to check his email, but he'd gone immediately into his address book to see who was online at the moment, and he had only looked for one name. Suddenly, he felt as if he were spying, and he logged off, hoping she hadn't seen his smiley face on her computer.

You know, it was unlocked all night, he said. He stood in the kitchen in his pajamas, sipping on a vanilla coffee with whipped cream. How could you forget, he asked.

I don't know, she answered. I just forgot.

Three days later it happened again. She said no she wasn't trying to get it stolen, and he said it sure seemed like it. As they argued, they prepared a stuffed chicken in the toaster oven. They complemented it with a bottle of Médoc and broccoli with cheese sauce. That evening they picked at gauzy blue strands of cotton candy and talked about where they should go for their next Saturday drive.

What about the temple at Maisan, Geenie suggested. I've always thought I should make it to Maisan while I'm still here.

As she said those final words, while I'm still here, the cotton candy soured in L.B.'s stomach. What do you mean while you're still here, he asked, his voice shaking.

I don't know, she said, and her voice quivered, too.

He told her she must know, and she protested.

That night he lay looking at the ceiling, and she lay curled with her back to him, speaking to the wall as she told him about the job offer. She said she hadn't decided yet, and when he pushed for an answer, she only cried.

He tried to remember the last time they'd gone to bed without making love. He couldn't. Sometime in the night she rolled over, and when he woke just before dawn, her head was on his chest. Until well after sunup, he listened to her breathe and felt the smooth heat of her skin on his.

They skipped breakfast, and it was still early enough for them to feel the morning chill in the air as they drove out of town toward Maisan. The lowlands were especially cool, and the fog that lay over the fields smelled thickly of earth and vegetation.

As the morning mist lifted, they saw that the countryside had begun to change. Some of the rice paddies had been drained and harvested, brown stubble where the rice plugs had been reaped. Pumpkins swelled from the sides of raised walkways between the rice paddies, and the apples and pears, still on the trees, were individually wrapped in newspaper. The paper would insulate them from hungry insects and the warping power of the sun. The fruit would ripen behind its shroud, perfectly round and blemish free.

They ate their lunch beside the temple, and then spent the day walking hand-in-hand along mountain paths, eating grapes they'd bought at a roadside stand, and marveling at the steep cairns, the piles of prayer stones that rose up all around the temple.

That monk spent fifty years stacking these stones, L.B. said. He was reading the English half of an information plaque. Geenie stood in front of him and pushed her back into his chest as he held her in his arms. He slipped his fingers beneath the waistband of her pants and rested his palms low on her belly.

The guy didn't use any cement, he said. Or wires or anything.

Let's go to the top, she said.

You can't climb on them, he told her.

Not the rocks, silly. The mountain.

She pushed off of him, and he ran up the path after her.

L.B. saw the black sedan as it changed lanes behind them. They had waited to watch the sunset at Maisan, and when they hit the city limits, they'd found themselves locked into a small pocket surrounded by rush-hour traffic. So far back, seen through the waning light and the slight vibrations of his mirror, the car was just a black wisp, like smoke from burning plastic, as it slipped between two other cars. He looked for some opening in the traffic through which he might weave forward, but it was packed too densely. When he saw the car again, another hiss of black in his cat's-eye mirror, it was closer than before. The scooter swerved as L.B.'s muscles tensed.

What? Geenie said. Did you see it? She twisted left and right, trying to look behind her, her vision stifled inside the helmet.

It's there, he said. You can't see it right now.

What are we going to do?

It's stuck in traffic just like we are. It can't get to us.

Then why do you keep looking in the mirror? Stop it.

L.B. drove along with the current of traffic and strained to look straight ahead, his peripheral vision trying to cheat over to the mirror. He didn't look again until Geenie shouted. The car was directly behind them, its bumper lunging at their scooter as the driver moved his foot from gas to brake to gas.

The cars ahead and to the sides of the scooter were still locked together, and L.B. had nowhere to go. Geenie yelled over and over, do something do something, but there was nothing for him to do. He flowed along with traffic, powerless, as the car thrust toward their rear tire. He didn't think about running away anymore. He didn't think about hiding. He thought only of what he would do if he could get to that man in the black suit. Beat him into nothingness. Strangle him into thin air. He could feel the tendons of the man's neck fighting beneath his fingers, the pulse in the carotid artery strong then stopping. Engrossed in his imagination, he almost didn't notice when the car to his left turned on its blinker and slowed for a turn. He slipped into the newly opened space. The black car pulled up beside them, so close L.B. could reach out and touch it. A traffic light ahead turned red, and everything stopped.

For a moment L.B. stared at his yellow helmet reflected in the black driver's-side window, then he tore the helmet from his head, threw it at the car and beat with his fist on the tinted glass. As soon as it slid down enough to reach a hand in, he grabbed the top of the window and pulled. It shattered with a bang, and tiny fragments of glass dropped like a curtain of water falling between L.B. and the driver, a white-haired businessman whose hand shook at the steering wheel, and whose horrified eyes were locked with L.B.'s.

It's not real, Geenie said. She stood in L.B.'s living room.

That wasn't the right car, but it doesn't mean it's not out there.

I'm not just talking about that, she said. I mean everything. None of this is real.

What about our car, he asked, and he put his arms around her.

It's not a car, she said, pulling away. It's a fucking scooter. This isn't even our home. It's all just make-believe.

So what. It's our make-believe.

I can't stay in it any longer. Don't you see, L.B.? Where are we? Where did we go?

She said she needed a night away, and L.B. drove her home. He didn't trust leaving the scooter at her apartment overnight. As he pulled up to the curb, he saw the group of teenagers hanging out in the parking lot in front of her entrance, still in their school uniforms at ten p.m.

Do you want me to walk you up, he asked.

She looked at the teenaged boys. No, she said. I'm fine. Really.

As she walked toward them, one of the boys waved and said hello in English. She said hello back. She was still talking to them as L.B. drove away.

Just as he was drifting to sleep, sometime toward morning, L.B. thought he might have heard something, a sound like fingers typing on a keyboard, but sharper, more metallic, a hushed ringing of steel.

The next morning he stood in his parking lot with a broken chain in his hands. He wore the striped flannel pajamas that Geenie had bought him, and they soaked up the warmth from the sun. Just the slightest wisps of air, like a cold stream, curled pleasantly around his ankles and the back of his neck.

He was sitting in the parking lot with a cup of black coffee, still in his pajamas, when Geenie got out of a taxi in front of his apartment. She sat on the curb beside him. Neither of them looked in the direction of the bicycle rack.

I know I picked them out, she said, but you look a little silly in those pajamas.

It almost smells like snow this morning, he said.

It does. I like it.

He set his coffee cup on the pavement and put an arm around Geenie. Her jacket was cold.

Maybe it'll turn up, she said.

I hope not, he said.

Really? she asked.

Yeah, I think really.

He took another sip of coffee. She pinched up a piece of his flannel pajama top and rolled the fabric between her thumb and finger. So do I, she said. They looked at each other closely, and L.B. felt in his cheeks the same warmth that reddened hers. She smiled a little bit of a smile and looked down.

I accepted the job offer, she said.

I thought you would.

He pulled her close and kissed her tentatively, and then hard. Her lips were warm. She dug her fingernails into his back. Their teeth clicked together. They kissed for a long time, and there was nothing at all adorable in that kiss. It was not a kiss that would make one think of smiley faces or pinches that go beep. It wouldn't remind anyone of cotton candy or tenderized hams. Not flannel but the sound of tearing flannel. The crack of breaking plastic. The striking of a match.

RIDE THE COMET

Sexual desire triggered Larry's most acute bouts of heart-ache—though the sex was not really what his heart ached for—and masturbation brought his greatest depression, each hopeless ejaculation a microcosm of his life, now single at forty; beached whales, sharks lost in freshwater deltas, salmon trapped on the wrong side of the dam.

In these moments alone, as his tension mounted, he focused his mind straight ahead, using any tricks he could—Asians, Native Americans, Latinas, fat women, short women, black hair, red hair, green eyes, blue—anything to keep his vision from sneaking to the peripherals where he'd pushed nine years of Linda's sandy hair and curious brown eyes. For the four or five seconds of release—ten if he were lucky—between the heartache and the depression, he was there with himself in his hand, floating two inches off the bathroom floor, wrapped in a gauze of music, the final frenzied clash of "Zorba's Dance" giving way to the weightlessness of "The Blue Danube Waltz." Away he floated, mouth open, hardly long enough even to hope he never came down.

When he did descend, he landed on cold tile beneath the flickering bare fluorescent bulb of a 1930s-era bath-room in his new apartment, a one-bedroom in a broken-up house in the city. He hadn't known how he would ever get through apartment hunting. He had stepped through the doors of so many one- and two-bedroom boxes, each still with the smell of shampoo and floor wax and dogs and cats and cigarettes and spaghetti, a long straight hair still clinging to a tub, its tail down the drain, the back of an earring lost in the dust on a window sill.

Light. That's what his aunt Penn had told him. Look for lots of light. When she walked through his apartment door for the first time, she said only, "Oh, Larry, what did you do?" She came back half an hour later carrying a floor lamp with three swiveling lights at the top, and she placed it next to him where he sat in a reclining chair beside an old record player. He'd found both the chair and the record player in the classified ads. A thirteen-inch black-and-white Zenith TV sat on the floor in front of him, also from the paper. "Soap operas and game shows," Penn said. "That's no good. I'm taking it." And she did.

The first thing he'd bought for his new apartment had been a phone and an answering machine. After that, he'd bought a Hoover upright vacuum cleaner that he still hadn't used. He'd gone to Sears and, knowing nothing about vacuums, had listened to the saleswoman detail the features of several models. He was giving her the money for a bagless with a HEPA filter when he felt her hand on his forearm. She wore a wedding band, and her fingers were lined from years of worrying over limed sinks and scuffed floors. He looked from that plain honest hand to her eyes, eyes so like her hand, like a helpless wringing of hands.

"I just can't take it," she said, as she gave Larry back the two extra twenties he'd given her. "I had a man in here yesterday, and I can't stop thinking about the cook-set he bought. Twelve pieces. He'll never even take it out of the box. You poor things."

He knew then he couldn't again step foot into another household goods department, small appliances store, kitchenware, or linen store. When he got home with the vacuum cleaner, he watched, as he always did, the steady red light on the answering machine.

After Penn left with the TV, Larry cued up Zorba's Dance and mouthed the intro along with the actors' voices. "Teach me to dance, will you?" Basil asked, tentatively.

"Did you say . . . *dance*?!" Zorba replied, exuberantly. "Come on, my boy!"

Larry stepped into the bathroom in time with the first slow notes, and for three and a half minutes he worked himself faster and faster into a lather beneath the flickering light. He weighed anchor with the last note and stomp of Zorba's feet; the next record dropped, and as the cellos opened The Blue Danube, he rose this time up and out of his bathroom. He floated over the streetlights of his neighborhood, up and over the twinkling city, and there, spinning slowly, watched amazed as a steady trickle of men, pants around their ankles, spiraled lazily up around him, like fireflies. A man with white hair and delicate thighs floated past, gazing, bewildered, into a double boiler.

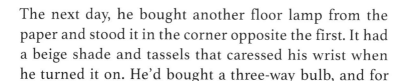

The next day, he bought another floor lamp from the paper and stood it in the corner opposite the first. It had a beige shade and tassels that caressed his wrist when he turned it on. He'd bought a three-way bulb, and for several minutes he clicked it from one brightness to the next, testing every combination between that lamp and the lamp that Penn had bought him. He settled on the lowest setting on the tasseled lamp, and two of the three lights on the other, one pointing at the ceiling and the other down at his lap.

"Congratulations," Penn said that evening. "I'm proud of you, Larry. Now when are you going to go back to work? Bill wants to stop coverage on his boat for the winter."

Larry swiveled the lowest light on Penn's lamp half an inch to the left.

"I wish you'd talk to me," Penn said. "This isn't healthy."

He clicked off the lamp.

"Larry, you know I love you. I feel for you, I really do, but sooner or later this has to end. I'm going to do your dishes."

"They fired me," he said.

"Really?" she asked, pausing on her way to the kitchen. "No. They didn't fire you, Larry. You just stopped. You did. You really did."

There weren't many dishes to do. He'd bought just two of everything necessary from St. Luke's Thrift Store. He had two plates, two bowls, two glasses, and two of each utensil. He had a saucepan and a cast-iron frying pan permanently on his stove. He had a spatula and a wooden spoon.

After Penn left, Larry circled garage sales in the paper, and the next day he picked up an end table and yet another floor lamp, this one splaying into multi-colored fiber-optic threads. He put it behind his chair where it arced over his head like a little firework. He'd also bought a record at a yard sale, the soundtrack from the movie *Ordinary People* starring Donald Sutherland and

Mary Tyler Moore, and featuring Pachelbel's *Canon in D* and Handel's *Messiah*, "Hallelujah" chorus. The man who sold it to him was middle-aged and dark-skinned with white hair creeping up his temples.

"My wife played cello," the man said, standing in his front yard, pieces of their life like bones around him.

"I love the cello," Larry said.

"So did I," the man said.

Larry gave him a dollar for the record. The man gave him back fifty cents.

When Larry returned home, his answering machine light was blinking. The message was ten seconds of silence.

"King of kings!" the Mormon Tabernacle Choir shouted. "And Lord of lords! He shall reign forever and ever! Hallelujah! Hallelujah! Hallelujah!" And Larry was gone, wrapped this time in sacrilege, blasted off with endorphins, and finding a stable orbit over the city with the opening bass notes of Pachelbel's canon. He didn't see the record's previous owner that night over the twinkling lights, though he looked for him among the crowd of men, gyroscopes, spinning slowly around themselves in the amber glow. But as he descended he caught the attention of a woman with her hand between her naked legs, hips darting. Their eyes met for what seemed a long time, but the only description Larry could conjure an hour later was that of the expression on the face of the man who'd sold him the record, the look in his eyes as he'd held out the fifty cents change.

Moving from the household goods section of the classified ads, Larry found the events section and began showing up at this or that community affair. He went to craft shows in the park. He went to flea markets. He visited soup kitchens, where he sometimes volunteered and sometimes just sat down and ate. And at all these places he saw the shocked and the dazed. He watched the slow rolling eyes and listened to the shy faltering utterances of people suspended in disbelief—separated, widowed, divorced, broken. And each evening he dropped his keys on his end table and stared at the steady red light on his answering machine.

He went one Saturday evening to the public library, where he sat through their children's story hour, boys and girls in flannel pajamas scattered like jacks across the floor while the librarian read. When she finished, she asked Larry if he'd like to read on the following Saturday. "The poor man," she said to a mother as Larry walked toward a shelf in the children's section, where he would agonize for two days over which story to read. "He must have lost a child."

Larry sat on a metal chair and read to the children: "The matches glowed with a light that was brighter than the noon-day." Here he struck a wooden match. "And it smelled so deliciously of roast goose. Her grandmother had never appeared so large or so beautiful. She took the little girl in her arms, and they both flew upwards in brightness and joy far above the earth, where there was neither cold nor hunger nor pain, for they were with God."

The match snuffed out at Larry's fingertips while the little match girl froze to death on the sidewalk, and as the smoke trickled up, two girls in the front grabbed each other and burst into tears. The librarian blew her nose into a damp Kleenex, looked around the room at the sniffling children, and clapped uneasily.

Larry came home to find his answering machine's light blinking again, another message of silence. He listened to it several times.

On Sunday, he sat down with the paper and flipped through the City Life section. He saw that the autumn county fair was a week away, and that Art Fest was coming up. He saw an ad for a skywatch party at Milham Park. They would be watching the Leonid meteor shower, the debris from the Tempel-Tuttle comet. "Come after midnight," the ad said, "when the Western Hemisphere will be riding on the front of Earth's orbit and facing directly into the storm." He also found that a local used car dealership was open that day for a hunting-season special, giving away a free shotgun and a frozen turkey to the first fifty people who test-drove a car. He slicked back his hair with water, put on a tie, and drove to the car dealer.

Getting no preference from Larry, the salesman put him in a Ford Explorer. He said that while Larry was out, they'd appraise his trade-in, a rusting Toyota that had been a second car. Larry took the Ford out of the city, wandering along back roads and looking at country houses set among patches of red and orange trees. On the way back to the dealership, he bought earplugs and shotgun shells—slugs, each shell containing a single marble-sized ball of lead. He told the car salesmen he'd think about his offer, put the gun and the turkey into his trunk, and drove out of town.

He drove through the countryside until he found a power line, which he followed to a dirt two-track that ran beneath the wires. At a bowl-shaped clearing, he parked the car, loaded the shotgun, pushed in his earplugs, and carried the turkey to the far slope. He walked back toward his car, turned, and took aim.

His first shot tore out a crater of sand two feet to the left of the turkey. He pumped the stock clumsily, and the smoking shell arced off to his right. He aimed again. The slug hit, and the turkey exploded. Shards of frozen bird, like pieces of china, rained down as the sound of the blast echoed through the woods and fields. Larry smiled, a feeling in his chest like the ejected shell that flipped smoking through the air, landing by the first—two spent shells in the sand. He watched them until the last trickle of smoke rose from the newest. It didn't take long, and he wanted to believe that that was good. Fires die, he thought. But looking from the empty shells to the pieces of turkey, he wasn't so sure. "And what was still more wonderful," he'd read to the children at the library, "the goose jumped down from the dish and waddled across the floor, with a knife and fork in its breast, to the little girl. Then the match went out, and there remained nothing but the thick, damp, cold wall before her."

Larry bought a spring-loaded skeet thrower and a box of clay pigeons, and he drove to the power lines every morning that week, shooting through boxes of ammunition until he could knock down two discs thrown together—firing, pumping, and firing again before the second clay pigeon hit the ground. He shot until his finger was sore. He shot until his shoulder was bruised, until his left arm was stiff and heavy from raising the gun and working the pump. And when he came home, he lit up the house and looked at the little red light on his answering machine, some days glowing steadily, and some days blinking to announce so many seconds of silence.

The county ran a full-page ad in the paper the day the autumn fair opened—livestock judging, bake-offs, free warm cider and hot chocolate, rides and games, a motor-cycle stunt show, and a demolition derby. Larry spent the first day mostly in the barns, smelling the hay and watching the animals. The horses took to him, nuzzling their velvet noses against his neck, and turning sideways to present him with their enormous teardrop eyes.

In the afternoon, Larry watched the stunt cycle jump cars and buses, the rider doing wheelies and handstands on the bike as he circled the track between jumps. As the sun set, Larry rode the Ferris wheel. While he waited at the top for the carny to load more passengers, the lights came on, colored neon all around him blinking to life, a watercolor wash on everyone at the fair. He rode more rides, spinning and flipping until his stomach grew queasy, and then he walked along the midway, its dancing lights like shouting voices. Now and then he stopped to throw darts at balloons or squirt water into a clown's mouth. He was about to leave, the desire to look at the answering machine gnawing at his chest, when he found, at the far end of the avenue of games, the skeet-shoot booth. Hung in the back of the booth was a movie screen painted with a silhouette of trees. The guns shot at disks of light that flew across the screen.

"You're kidding me," Larry said as he looked at the prizes—lava lamps, Japanese lanterns, neon lights, black lights, Christmas lights, Halloween lights, nightlights, and glow-in-the-dark stickers.

A thin woman leaned against the counter, her hands stuffed into her money pouch. Her hair was flat and colorless, her face hard and lined. "No kidding here," she said. "One dollar, twenty shots, twelve or more hits gets you a prize."

Larry gave her a dollar and picked up a shotgun. He hit eight on his first try, still dizzy from the rides and unused to the gun.

"You don't have to pump it, sugar," the woman said. "Just pull the trigger."

He hit ten with his second dollar.

"You sure like to pump that thing, don't you," she said.

He hit thirteen with his third dollar, and she gave him a choice of four glow-in-the-dark stickers. He chose Saturn. He played four more times, the last time hitting eighteen and winning a string of orange patio lights in the shape of Frank Lloyd Wright houses. When he came home, the answering machine was blinking double for two messages.

The first was his Aunt Penn. "Where the hell are you, Larry? I'm worried about you. I saw your gun. What does that mean?"

The second was a long silence, longer this time than any of the others, and ending with a muffled sound that might have been a sigh, or might have been a sob. He replayed the message a dozen times, reading in that single sound entire essays, memoirs, apologies, and explanations. He played it again and again until the stories turned back upon themselves, convoluted and contradictory and, finally, meaningless.

The big attraction the next day was the demolition derby at sundown. The stands were full and raucous as the field turned slowly into a smoking auto graveyard. The winner stood shirtless on a podium, his belly hanging over his belt and his sweat steaming in the cool air as he shook a forty-ounce bottle of beer and sprayed it over his head. The crowd went nuts. Larry stepped down the bleachers and into the midway.

"Back for more, Pumper?" the skeet-shoot carny said.

He put a fifty-dollar bill on the counter and picked up a gun.

"I don't have change for this," she said.

"I won't need it."

"Shoot away," she said through a cigarette, shielding her lighter with her palm.

An hour and a half later, she helped him box up his winnings, an assortment of lamps, strings of lights, and a pile of stickers.

"The boss isn't going to like this," she said.

Their hands touched as she handed him the box.

Throughout the evening, as he'd racked up his winnings, her demeanor had changed. She stood a little taller, tucked a lock of hair behind her ear, displayed his prizes with a little bob of her hips.

"See you tomorrow night?" she asked as he left.

"I suppose," he said.

The last night of the fair, before shooting skeets, he took another round on the rides. He bought a string of tickets and worked his way from the Matterhorn to the Recoil to the Barrel Roll to the Comet, where he found himself alone. He locked down the bar, and the ride spun to life, whipping him until his hip ached from being forced into the metal side of the carriage. Two or three minutes passed as he strained to hold himself away from that biting edge. Another minute passed, and then another. He whipped toward the operator, and as he paused for a half-second at the apex of the arc, he saw the man on his stool, arms crossed on the console, head on his arms, sleeping soundly. On the next pass, Larry yelled, but the noise of the ride overwhelmed his voice. He continued to yell anyway, each time he passed close. His head throbbed and grew heavy, and he felt himself sliding backward down a hole. The light of the world grew smaller and smaller until it was a pinprick far away at the hole's opening. Then it disappeared altogether.

Larry walked down a cobblestone street in the light of a few gas lamps. A horse-drawn carriage clattered by. Snow drifted against the sides of buildings, and the stones shone with a film of frost. In one hand he held his shotgun, in the other, the hand of a little barefoot girl. She carried a bundle of matches, carefully, as another child might carry a cupcake. She led him down the street to a small alcove beside the front steps of an apartment building, and there they huddled together, while she worked a match from the bundle with stiff fingers and struck it against the stone wall. The match flared, and the wall grew transparent in the yellow light. The Christmas tree from her story was there in the apartment, and the table decked out with a New Year's Eve holiday feast, a goose on a platter in the center. "See?" the little match girl said, pointing, and the goose stood up, the carving knife and fork stuck in its abdomen. But it wasn't a goose at all. It was Linda, her curious brown eyes looking out through the wall.

Larry opened his mouth to speak, but she was once again a headless goose. With her nubbed wings, she pulled the knife and fork from her body and began to carve herself, laying slices of her flesh on the dinner plates around her. Then she dropped the fork and knife, lay on her back, and reached a wing between her legs. "The Christmas lights rose higher and higher," the little match girl said, "till they looked to her like the stars in the sky. Then she saw a star fall, leaving behind it a bright streak of fire. 'Someone is dying,' thought the little girl." The match went out, and the stone wall reappeared. Larry and the little match girl looked at each other. She looked down at her legs. Her toes were already black, her feet two deep bruises, and her ankles a beautiful sapphire blue. Larry put the barrel of the shotgun into his mouth and pulled the trigger.

"Mister. Hey mister," the carny was saying from the far end of the hole, as Larry sped back toward consciousness. "Are you okay? I'm sorry. I've been on the job since dawn. God, I'm sorry."

Larry didn't know how long he'd been out, or how long he'd been conscious again. "It's okay," he said. "Where am I?"

"Oh, Jesus," the carny said, looking up and down the lane. "Look. You're okay. You won't say anything, will you?"

"What? No . . . no. Say something? No."

Larry was fifty yards from the ride before he realized where he was. He remembered seeing his wife. He thought he remembered them making love. The fair came slowly into focus around him, the din of sound clearing into voices and bells and whistles. He stood still in the center of the midway, trying to remember where he'd been going. People stared as they walked by. The skeet shoot, he remembered, and walked first in the wrong direction, and then turned around.

The skeet-shoot carny's hair was lightly curled. She wore lipstick, a white silken blouse, and a short black skirt.

"Welcome back," she said. "Miss me?"

"Miss? Who? What are you talking about?" Larry said.

"Okay, okay," she said, pulling at the hem of her skirt. "It's just a joke, all right." She waved a hand at the shotguns. "Go ahead, Pumper, shoot your heart out."

After ten dollars' worth, Larry hadn't won anything.

"How about a shot of whatever you've been drinking," the carny said.

"I haven't been drinking," Larry said. "I fell asleep. I think I fell asleep. Somebody fell asleep."

"Well, in that case, then," she said, and she pulled a pint flask from beneath the counter. It made a small whistling sound as the whisky bubbled into her mouth. "Join me?" she asked.

He took a drink from the flask and handed it back. The warmth from the whiskey felt good against the cool night, and he relaxed and won a glow-in-the-dark sticker in his next turn.

"Now you're warming up," she said, and she took another drink.

As they walked to her trailer an hour later, Larry had a neon sign in the shape of a smoking cigarette under one arm, a Mickey Mouse nightlight under the other, and stickers falling out of his shirt pocket. "I want to show you something," she'd said when the fair had closed. She held the flask to his mouth as they walked, and he crouched to drink from it. She laughed and he laughed, and whiskey spilled down his neck and under his shirt.

Her trailer was black with two small windows near the top, looking as if it might have been made for horses. She opened the door. "You first," she said. He stepped up, into the blackness, and she followed, closing the door behind her. "Ready?" she said.

"Shit. What?" Larry said. "Ready for what?"

She flipped the light switch, and they were bathed in the light of dozens of lamps, neon and liquid and spar-kling. "I might as well enjoy them," she said.

He turned, and she kissed him.

He fell backward onto her bed and closed his eyes, dizzy from the whiskey and still sick from the ride. She did most of the work while he recovered, and when he finally opened his eyes, he and the carny were floating over the fairground, the city surrounding them, the air filled with copulating couples. He saw the woman who'd sold him his vacuum cleaner, now on her knees in front of a thin man in glasses who looked as if he'd just come in from gardening. He saw the man with the graying hair who'd sold him the record—he was crouched gently over a middle-aged woman, her fingers on his back long and elegant, just right for strings. Larry noticed that a piece was missing from the back of the man's head, and he looked away. He saw the librarian, head to toe with another woman. He saw a tanned man wearing a gold chain, spanking a young woman as he took her from behind. He saw costumes and bondage and food and toys.

Then he saw his wife. She lay on her back, looking far up into the night sky while a man sweated on top of her.

"We break camp at dawn," the carny said, and they were back in her trailer. She was up and putting on her bra and underwear, elastic bands snapping and little plastic hooks clipping. "It was nice, though."

"Where are you going?"

"Another fairground, sugar. They're all the same."

It was two a.m. when Larry got home. His answering-machine light was blinking in a series of three. The first message was from Penn. "Larry, damn it, call me." The next was also from Penn. "Larry. I need to talk to you. It's about Linda."

The third message started with silence, and then Linda's voice. At the sound of it, Larry remembered a dozen things at once, Christmases and anniversaries, a bungalow in Costa Rica, broiled whitefish they'd learned to cook together. "Larry," she said. "I can't do this anymore. It's too hard. I won't call again. The lawyers can handle it. Goodbye, Larry."

He stood still for several minutes after the beep. The phone rang, and he jumped. It was Penn. "Jesus, Larry, it's about time. I've been calling all night. Are you okay, Lar?"

"Linda called."

"I wanted to warn you, Larry. I couldn't reach you."

"It's okay."

"No, it's not. It's shitty."

"She never told me why, Penn."

"I don't think she knew."

"Maybe I could have done something."

"I don't know, Lar. I'm not so sure."

"Just before she left, she was working on the car," Larry said. "I keep thinking about it."

"Oh, Lar," Penn said.

"She wanted to install the new alternator. She ordered the parts and bought a book. She put on overalls and went into the garage. When she came back in, her face was streaked with grease. We stood there in the living room looking toward each other but not at each other. Looking at something in the air between us. And I remember thinking that if I slid my arms through the sides of her overalls, she would be right there, and if I did that, then that thing between us would go away."

Larry looked at the unlit lamps around his chair. "Why didn't I do it, Penn?" he asked. "Why didn't I do something? Why didn't she?"

Penn was quiet, and Larry breathed into the phone, winded and unused to talking. "I have to go," he said.

"I'll come by in the morning," she said. "I'll fix you breakfast."

He drove to Milham Park. Fifty or more people were gathered in a large clearing looking at the night sky. Most lay on lawn chairs, covered with blankets or wrapped in sleeping bags. A few milled between telescopes. Larry walked into the clearing and looked up. The sky was a barrage of shooting stars, the debris left behind by the Tempel-Tuttle comet, half a dozen meteors streaking over the crowd at any one time. Most were thin white lines, but now and then one shot by orange and jagged, and he could see the fire in it. People oohed and aahed at the brighter ones. They cheered and clapped at the brightest. A few minutes passed while he stood and watched the show, and then a big one crashed into the air, a bright red flame ripping across the sky. A great cheer arose as it arced over the people's heads, and Larry was lifted off the ground, catapulted up toward the streaks of light. Higher and higher he flew until he shot out of sight, leading the way as the planet turned its naked face toward the storm and punched, a thousand miles a minute, through the tail of the comet.

A RABBIT
FOR ALYOSHA

Alyosha had just dialed his daughter's telephone number when he saw the dog, a shaggy brown thing standing on the sidewalk in front of his house. He had punched Kaleena's number into a cordless handset with his thumb, reading the digits aloud from a yellowed slip of paper. His call was to be a birthday greeting. As the telephone rang, he stood on the cement stoop of his brick bungalow, the receiver to his ear, and he and the strange dog looked at each other from either side of the yard.

Alyosha's granddaughter, Molly, answered. He asked Molly how she was, and she grunted. He asked how school was, and she said okay. He asked what grade she was in, and she snorted through her nose, a static of wind in the receiver, and said, Sixth? Hello? He asked to speak with her mother, and the receiver fell onto a countertop.

The birthday call to Kaleena was one day early. Alyosha had wished her an early happy birthday ever since her sixth, when he and Marta had decorated the kitchen for a surprise party, convinced that the day was October fifteenth, when, in fact, it had only been the fourteenth.

As he waited for his daughter to come to the telephone, Alyosha thought that this would be the day that he would finish his yard work. He had chosen a stretch of three beautiful autumn days for the job, the skies so deep over his head that when he looked long enough he thought he could see the blackness of space beyond. He looked often at the cloudless sky as he worked, his grip on the handle of the rake tightening each time he looked up, his faith in gravity wavering. There seemed too little between himself and that depth of sky.

The crabapple tree in his front yard had weeks earlier dropped both its leaves and its fruit. Now, only a pie-shaped wedge of litter remained beneath its bare branches, Alyosha having cleared the rest of the circle of debris over the previous two days. He had only that wedge of crabapples to finish, and the flower beds that ran along the front of his house. The beds lay thick with maple and ash leaves, blown in from neighbors' trees and from the woods that began at the end of the cul-de-sac. The lawns of his neighbors' houses had already been raked clean, square patches of green in front of the small brick homes that ran in neat lines on either side of the white street. Each day as he had worked in the yard, he had told himself that he would finish that day with the flower beds. But each evening, he had been too exhausted to pick the mat of leaves from the beds, his shoulder too sore from the fight with the crabapples, those knotted little fists that rolled through the tines of his rake.

His exhaustion was mental, too, his nerves frayed from the torment of sweat bees that welled up from the rotting apples each time he came out for another hour with the rake. On his first day in the yard, a bee had been ensnared by the frayed gray hairs of his beard and had stung him on the cheek. Yes, the yard work had been a disappointment, he acknowledged, spoiled by the bees and also by the reluctance of his body. He had enjoyed the first day well enough despite the bees, but he had awoken the next morning in pain. Not the satisfying stiffness of muscles, but a deep ache in his joints. His shoulder pained him so this morning, that he had been unable to lift his arm to pull a coffee mug from the cupboard.

The dog's head is too big, Alyosha thought, as he saw how the head hung below the dog's shoulders as if it were a burden. He saw also that the dog held something in its mouth, something brown and white and plush—a stuffed toy, he guessed. He could not see if the dog wore a collar or tags. They could be lost beneath the fur, which draped itself over the dog's body in long layers, each a different shade of brown, fur so thick that the dog's front legs looked like a single pedestal. They looked this way, that is, until the dog lifted its front left paw and, its heavy head still trained on Alyosha, placed a furry foot on the edge of his lawn.

A long time passed as Kaleena's telephone receiver lay on the countertop of what Alyosha assumed was her kitchen. When he spoke on the telephone to Kaleena, he always pictured her on the kitchen phone in the tall and narrow house by the brewery, though she had moved away from that house when she married John, and Alyosha had reluctantly sold it three years ago, only half admitting to himself that he had become too old to keep the place up. He had seen Kaleena once since he'd moved into the brick bungalow, when she'd visited with Molly and John. She had told him that they would come for three days, but it hadn't gone well. They sat for most of the visit in his living room struggling to find points of conversation. The only topic Alyosha could think to address to John was the fact of John being a vegetarian. When, during lunch the second day, he asked John for the third time—You don't think you're worth a chicken?—Kaleena said they were leaving early. The chicken comment had not been the whole problem, Alyosha knew. Molly had slouched back in a chair in the living room the entire time, arms drooped over the sides of the chair, head back as if she were dying of heat or of hunger. Kaleena had bitten her nails continuously, and when Alyosha talked of Marta—the only topic he could think to address to her—he had seen the muscles in her jaw pulse. When he asked, Do you remember your mother, Kaleena? She asked him, Do you ever not?

Through the receiver, Alyosha heard Molly yelling for her mother. Telephone, the girl said. Not *dedushka*, not *ded*, not even Grandpa. Telephone. He could be anybody. He should have remembered what grade the girl was in. He should not have had to ask. Okay, he had forgotten her precise age. But he did remember the night Molly was born, his arrival at Saint Helen's Hospital two hours after her birth, an arrival that brought him there technically on the following day, as she had been born an hour before midnight. December twenty-second. The shortest day of the year. Alyosha's son-in-law had already filled in the name on the birth certificate. Molly Anne Brown.

Molly. The name ran often through Alyosha's mind. It could not be avoided. There were Mollies his granddaughter's age everywhere. The name was, he learned, the most popular girl's name in the year of his granddaughter's birth. Kaleena wasn't obligated to choose a Russian name, he told himself. She had never even been to Russia, had never seen the city gate at Severodvinsk. But the most popular name in America?

Molly. He thought of a girl in lavender sitting at a wooden desk, her hair tied with satin bows into two pigtails. He thought of her staring at her teacher, excited and vacant. Around her a roomful of Mollies, each eager to say what she thought the teacher would want to hear. A roomful of Mollies all wanting the same blond-haired boy. All fluffed in petticoats and crinoline at the prom. All pliable and submissive in sex. All marrying drunkards and fools. It didn't have to be a Russian name. But there is something in a name. Give her a name with some power to it. A name that carries a sense of command. Katya. Elziveta. Zinalda. Well, maybe it did have to be a Russian name. If Marta had still been here, he thought, she would not have allowed John to name her granddaughter Molly.

Molly. Mopey. Mushy. Muffy. The dog hadn't moved since testing its paw in Alyosha's lawn. Muffy, Alyosha said. Where have you sprung from, Muffy? The dog dipped its heavy head and brought it up, a gesture that had not always been so slow, Alyosha thought, a playful tossing of its mane. The plush thing in the dog's mouth didn't flop with the tossing of its head, but poked out stiffly to either side. The dog chewed on it, letting it almost drop, before clenching it again in its teeth. A curled brown foot flashed, and then disappeared under the dog's lip. A squirrel? Alyosha wondered. As he studied the thing, looking for the tail, the dog picked its front right foot off the sidewalk and set it, too, down on the grass.

Kaleena sounded distracted when she said hello. She didn't know who was on the other end of the line, and Alyosha heard the voice she used for strangers—guarded, firm. She had a good name. A Kaleena can take care of herself in this world.

It's me, Alyosha said. Papa. Happy birthday.

Thanks, Papa.

Is your John taking you somewhere for your birthday?

We're going to the coast.

Good. That's good.

Yeah, I think so.

Yes.

Yeah.

Good. Good, good.

Alyosha nodded his head, and the bristle of his beard slid against the receiver. Kaleena would not recognize his beard. Marta had never known him with a beard. In the thirty-five years of their marriage, she had not known more than the three day's worth of stubble he would have after his weekly trip over the bridge.

For thirty years he drove each week across the Mackinaw Bridge, hauling five hundred cases of beer from the brewery in Chippewa Falls, Wisconsin, across the upper peninsula of Michigan, to a distribution warehouse in Mackinac City. One day over, one day unloading the beer, reloading Vernor's ginger ale, and one day to return. He would walk home from the brewery at two a.m. after unloading the ginger ale. He would enter the house through the kitchen, and Marta would be there, sitting in a chair on one side of their square metal table, the other chair for him. Between them would rest a loaf of pumpernickel, a knife and sausage on a plate, and a quart of beer into which she had dropped a raw egg, the yolk sliding down the thin neck, a tuft of foam rising above the brown glass lip.

As he ate he would tell her about the deer he had almost hit, or the coyote. He would tell her how Pearl Dombrowski was getting on without her husband to help her manage the warehouse in Mackinac City. He would tell his wife how he had thought of her waiting for him in this kitchen, how that thought kept him awake at the wheel. I could smell the sausage, he would say. Some weeks he pushed the metal table aside and waltzed her around the kitchen, his calloused hand rough on the small of her back, his kiss forceful—beer and sausage and a three-day beard. Marta described this scene often to the young women with whom she worked in the bottling room. The touch of a man, she would say to the women. Skinny little boys they married, she would say to Alyosha.

When Marta became pregnant with Kaleena at age forty-eight, she displayed her round belly to the young women in the bottling room. They don't make men like my Yosha anymore, she said. Nor women like you, the young women said. Marta swelled with pride when they said this, her strong forearms crossed over her belly. And if, when Marta turned her back, the young women asked among themselves if last month she wasn't thirty-eight, Marta didn't mind. Let them remember me when they're forty-eight, she told Alyosha.

Only at night did Marta fear, curled into Alyosha's thick side, moonlight shining off the brass bars of their bed. I think I'm too old, she would say. Hush, Alyosha would say, look at the women here who have babies. Pigeons. You're worth three of them. God has given us a gift, Marta.

The dog had crept to the middle of the lawn, where it stood in the broken shade of the bare crabapple tree.

A cotton ball of white fur bloomed from beneath its lip, and Alyosha saw that the dead thing in its mouth was a rabbit. He remembered the rabbits they had kept at the old house by the brewery. He hadn't thought of them in a long time, and they hopped pleasantly in his mind. He thought of the hutch that he'd built of wood and chicken wire, doubting that he could do such a task again even if the rabbit in Muffy's mouth were alive. He remembered how Kaleena used to play with one of the rabbits. What did she call it? He couldn't remember.

Do you remember the rabbits? he asked into the telephone.

The rabbits? Kaleena said, and Alyosha could hear in her voice the same jaw-clenching tightness he had seen in his living room during her visit.

Remember how they bred? he asked. He felt as if he were tugging at her arm now, and he told himself not to pull too hard, though he wanted very much to pull her back to the old house, to the grass on a sunny day with her pet bunny.

Yes, I remember the rabbits, Kaleena said. Are you eating okay? Do you need anything?

We started with four, and by spring we must have had forty.

I don't really want to talk about the rabbits.

What did you call the one? The little one with the orange and white fur?

I don't know.

You used to play with it on the grass, on a sunny day.

I don't remember its name, Pop. It doesn't matter.

Tell Molly that I remember the day she was born. I just don't know the grades and the school years anymore. She's in sixth grade.

Going on twelfth. Did she get smart with you? She's been such a shit lately.

That bunny was smaller than the rest.

I don't know, Pop. I don't remember.

It was old? There was something about that one.

Do you have food in the house?

I'm okay, Kaleena.

Because I was talking with John.

I'm okay.

He agreed that if you needed to—if somday you really needed us to—we could probably make some room.

You don't need to make room.

I don't know where we'd put Molly. John's been talking about finishing off the basement. I'll believe that when I see it.

Alyosha imagined John in the basement, standing befuddled over a pile of two-by-fours, a hammer limp in his hand. John Brown. Only Smith would have made his name any more ordinary. Then Alyosha imagined John's father, the man who named John, standing befuddled beside his son as they looked together at the pile of lumber. The father finally speaking: Well, Son, we tried.

You don't need to move Molly, Alyosha told his daughter.

I would. It's not that I wouldn't. If you really needed to be with family. It just wouldn't be easy.

No, it wouldn't be easy.

Damn it, Papa, you don't make it— No. Never mind. I'm not going to do this.

Don't worry, Kaleena. I'm not as old as you imagine.

How old is the dog, Alyosha wondered. The fur around its mouth was gray, a soft cloud around the dead rabbit. Alyosha looked the dog over and realized that it was larger than he had earlier thought. It was enormous. One eye showed, brown and wet through a part in the shaggy locks that hung across its face. He felt the eye still on him as the dog lowered itself onto the lawn, first its hind quarters, then its front. Its fur fanned across the grass as it settled onto its belly. It's like something from the sea, Alyosha thought. Happy birthday, Kaleena, he told his daughter. Don't forget to tell Molly that I remember.

Alyosha sat on the edge of his cement porch. Muffy, he said. What are your intentions? The dog pushed with its hind legs, and its belly slid forward, its eye still on Alyosha. Then it dropped the rabbit, flopped onto its side and unfolded its tongue onto the grass.

Alyosha laid the phone on the stoop and walked toward the rabbit. A dozen feet away, he saw that the rabbit was moving. Half a dozen feet, and he saw its fur undulating, an unnatural animation of flesh. Closer, and he saw it roiling. Something white flashed in the dry crack of its mouth, and he thought dumbly of a baby tooth. The white thing fell to the lawn, a plump maggot that arched its back and corkscrewed into the grass. Oh Muffy, Alyosha said. What have you found?

He took a dustpan from the garage, and he slipped its rusting tin edge beneath the rabbit. With the rake, he slid the carcass onto the dustpan. The body felt light as he carried it to the garage. It felt like nothing. Nothing but hide and worms. He shook open a brown paper grocery bag, set it on the garage floor and tipped the dustpan over it. The carcass slid from the pan, food scraps sliding from a cutting board. But his aim was off, and the rabbit hit the lip of the bag. The paper folded under, and the carcass fell onto the garage floor, a scattering of maggots on the concrete, flung from a hole in the rabbit's hide.

"*Blyat*," Alyosha said. He looked toward the street, as if to find someone, to point out how he had been wronged, but no one was there to sympathize. The dark, thick scent of decay rose up, and he closed his mouth against it. Better to endure the smell of the bad air than to take it into his mouth. The brown paper of the bag's side was wet, a few white larvae clinging to its surface, lost on that desert. He slid the dustpan beneath the rabbit once more, touching the knurled spine with two fingers, holding the body still as the edge of the dustpan knifed under it. Then he lifted the bag open and placed the rabbit inside. Half a dozen larvae squirmed on the rust-scabbed surface of the dustpan, and he banged them off and rolled the bag closed.

His heart thumped haltingly against his ribs as he carried the grocery bag to the garbage can at the end of his drive. A tired thing, he thought of his heart, and he imagined it inside himself, the gasping red face of an old man.

He dropped the paper bag into the garbage can and closed the lid. Sweat ran into his eyes, and he wiped the palm of his hand across his forehead, raised the front of his shirt, and sponged the moisture from his eyebrows and beard. The dog raised its head from the grass and watched him. Who is older, Muffy? Alyosha asked. You or me? How old am I in dog years? Twenty? Thirty? A young man, thirty years old, dancing with Marta in the kitchen. He let his shirtfront drop, and he cupped his hand around his mouth. Making love with Marta in the kitchen, he whispered.

The clatter of bicycles sounded from the road behind Alyosha as he picked up his rake, and he knew before he looked that it would be the Maysles, the young couple who lived with their son at the end of the cul-de-sac. They had come to his house three years earlier to welcome him to the neighborhood. Mrs. Maysle had given him a Tupperware container filled with chocolate chip cookies that he didn't eat. She had returned a week later for the Tupperware, but he had thrown it out along with the cookies. Threw it away? she had asked, incredulously. Like, in the garbage?

Both the Maysle parents waved at Alyosha as they passed. Their son, a chubby boy of five or six, rode on a half-bicycle that attached to his father's seat post. They all wore helmets, the parents in spandex biking shorts and Day-Glo yellow jerseys. Alyosha nodded once, his hand on the rake. The boy isn't old enough to ride his own bicycle? he asked the dog.

He worked for an hour with the rake, while the dog lay in the grass. For his lunch, he added sausage to a pot of *shchi*. He heated it on the stove and placed the pot on the same enameled metal table that he had shared with Marta. He still sometimes had conversations with her as he sat at this table. I don't know why Kaleena settles so, he would say. I don't know how to talk to Molly. How does one talk to a Molly? If you were still here, he would so often say. If only you were here.

He dipped black bread into the soup and held it just long enough to take some broth. Kaleena, too, had served him at this table, after Marta died. He had returned from his first trip over the bridge after his wife's death and had found Kaleena asleep in the opposite chair, his bread and sausage and beer waiting for him. She was eight years old. He had eaten the food and carried her to her bed. She did not wake up, and he slept in a hard-backed chair in her room. He had no bed of his own, he had thought that night. There were only Kaleena's bed and Marta's bed. For thirty-five years, he felt that he had been a visitor in his wife's bed. For some reason unknown to him she had wanted him there, despite his clumsiness, despite his snoring and his smell of sausage and beer, despite the toll he took on the springs that complained so loudly when he lay down.

I should not have allowed Kaleena to wait on me, he told the dog when he had finished his lunch and returned to his rake. The dog had risen to its stomach. It found a crabapple, sniffed at it, and took a tentative bite. She should not have tried to stay up at night, Alyosha said. She should have been outside playing with the other children during the day. But Marta was gone. And wasn't I gone three days each week? There was the laundry. There was the house to clean. The shopping. Was I so unreasonable?

He worked at the crabapples for only thirty minutes before he leaned the rake against the brick wall of his house, turned on the garden hose, and drank greedily. His shirt stuck to his back. His neck itched with debris from the raking. He turned off the spigot and sat again on the porch. Dog years, he said to Muffy. Would it be too much to ask? Every seven years, I grow one year older. Or is it vice versa? The dog propped its forelegs beneath itself, raised its haunches off the ground, and walked over to the discarded hose where it lapped three or four times at the diminishing trickle that flowed from the brass nozzle.

You're thirsty, Alyosha said. You want my water. That I can give you.

He turned on the water, and the dog took another dozen slow licks at the nozzle. When it had finished, it stood motionless, its heavy head hanging from its shoulders. Alyosha sat again on the step, and the dog followed him. It turned its back and sat carefully on his foot. The Maysles passed again, this time walking. Going for ice cream, Alyosha suspected.

Mr. Maysle waved. Looks like you're about finished with the yard, he said.

You have a dog! Mrs. Maysle exclaimed. How cute! What's his name?

Alyosha looked at the dog. Vyacheslav, he said.

Vacha . . . ?

Vyacheslav Yevgeniy.

Yev . . . Vacha . . . Vachaslon . . . Mrs. Maysle stammered, laughing.

Alyosha waved his hand at her dismissively. Muffy, he said.

Oh, Muffy. You're just so cute. And big!

What's the boy's name, Alyosha asked, and the Maysle boy moved behind his father.

Dominic, Mrs. Maysle said. Say hi to Mr. Chernov, Nicky.

The boy buried his face in the side of his father's buttock.

Dominic, Alyosha repeated. Your son has a good name.

It was his grandfather's, Mr. Maysle said. It's Greek.

Your name has history, Dominic, Alyosha said. Dominic of Osma. Dominic of Prussia. It is a good name.

We call him Nick, Mrs. Maysle said. Say thank you, Nicky.

The boy's face stayed buried in his father's buttock, and Alyosha wondered why Mr. Maysle didn't pull him away and stand him so that the boy faced his company. Mrs. Maysle looked around the yard. She smiled at Alyosha, and as he looked back at her, her smile wilted. I guess we'd better be getting along, she said, adding brightly, We're getting ice cream. Alyosha nodded once, and when another empty moment had passed Mrs. Maysle let out a giggle.

You would do well to call him Dominic, Alyosha said.

Mrs. Maysle looked at Alyosha, and then at her husband and back at Alyosha. We call him Nick, she said.

Alyosha shrugged. Suit yourself, he said.

Goodnight, Mr. Chernov, Mr. Maysle said, and the three continued down the sidewalk, Nick hiding himself from Alyosha in the shadow of his father's leg.

When Kaleena was Dominic's age, Alyosha said to the dog, she no longer carried her baby fat. She rode her own bicycle to town with her mother to buy groceries. She cared for the rabbits. He placed his hands flat on the cement stoop behind him, and as he leaned his weight back, a pain ripped through his shoulder, a slow tearing, some frayed thing inside there that he thought of as burlap, the passive image in his mind of wood and nails and that coarse cloth. Imagine if we had rabbits in this yard, he said. He gave the dog a suspicious glance. Live rabbits, he added. But the Joneses would complain. The Smiths. The Browns. The Maysles. All complaining. Only you and I would appreciate them, Muffy. You could chase them around the grass. Our days of catching them may be over. But if we worked together.

Alyosha thought fondly of the tall, narrow house with the rabbit hutch in the corner of the backyard. Every other Sunday, he told Muffy, we had roast rabbit for dinner. You've never tasted anything like Marta's roasted rabbit.

Alyosha's leg was warm where the dog's back pressed against him. Maybe we'll call it a day, he said. What do you think, Muffy?

The dog lifted its nose to the sky, the fur fell away from its face, and it looked at the old man through dark, liquid eyes. Alyosha lifted his head, and they both looked at the sky. There were still no clouds, only the rich clear blue that seemed to deepen as Alyosha looked into it. Would a cloud be so bad? he asked, and he stood and straightened himself and walked on stiff legs into the house.

When he came back out that evening, he brought a cup of tea with milk for himself and a chopped length of sausage on a plate for the dog. He sat on the edge of the porch and set the plate on the walk in front of him. The dog sniffed the sausage and became excited. It pushed a paw onto the lip of the plate, and the sausage spilled onto the cement. It licked twice at a piece, and then ate its dinner without pause. When it had finished, it bucked its head in Alyosha's direction as it had that morning, a gesture that Alyosha thought had once been precocious. Alyosha flicked his hand at the dog. Ha! he said, and the dog dropped its front legs to the ground, touching what Alyosha thought of as its elbows to the grass. The dog's tail wagged, and Alyosha shouted louder—Ha!

The dog's front feet patted the ground, and then the dog pushed itself up and bounded one time around the crabapple tree. When it returned, Alyosha shouted again—Ha!—and the dog galumphed once more around the tree. When it returned this time, Alyosha pushed himself up and galumphed after it. Three times they bounded and then struggled around the tree before Alyosha broke away for the porch and settled panting onto the step. The dog followed and stood in front of him, its wet brown eye again visible through a part in its fur. No more, Alyosha said when he had caught his breath. You've worn an old man out. He sipped on his now-tepid tea and felt on his face the heat of Muffy's panting. The dog's fur glowed golden in the warm light of the setting sun. We're not so old, Alyosha said. Not so much use, maybe, but not so old. As Alyosha finished his tea the dog walked to the front wall of the house and stood in the flower bed. One paw scraped across the leaves, and then another. Then the dog set to work, turning circles and pawing until it had hollowed out a bed. It dropped into the hollow and tucked its head under its tail.

Alyosha stayed on the porch until the neighborhood around him had dimmed to a charcoal gray, and the white street glowed palely in the twilight. As he stood to go inside, the dog's rear leg began to twitch. What are you dreaming of, Muffy? he asked the dog. Maybe you are a pup again, and you are chasing the rabbits.

Sometime in the night Alyosha awoke, the old gasper his chest pounding against his ribs. A scrap of dream lingered in his mind—the corpse of the rabbit, as big as Muffy, lying in her place in the flower bed. The scrap drifted away as Alyosha pulled the sheets from his body, and it was replaced by a vivid recollection. He was at the old house, Marta only weeks in the grave. He was walking around the rabbit hutch, a rabbit in one hand, a knife in the other. He held the rabbit by the ears, and it bucked and squealed. The other rabbits in the hutch squealed in reply. A hammer hung from the back wall. He took the hammer in one hand, and with the other he held the rabbit against a stained flat stone. He rapped once with the hammer on the side of the rabbit's head, a light tap so as not to crush the skull, and the rabbit convulsed under his hand.

When it grew still, he cut open its belly and with his fingers scooped out the organs. He sliced through the skin along the circumference of the rabbit's neck and all four ankles, and when he had finished his cuts he pulled a nail from the side of the hutch, one of a dozen nails that he had tapped a quarter-inch into the wood. He held the rabbit's head to the side of the hutch and drove the nail through the base of its skull into the wood behind. Then he gripped the hide at the neck and yanked down, tearing the pelt from the flesh in one clean jerk. As he reached into the tube of the rabbit's skin, the meated body dangling from the nail, he noticed two things—the orange and white fur, and Kaleena watching from the corner of the hutch.

He waited until five thirty that morning to call his daughter. He had spent the intervening hours sitting at the enameled metal table, drinking the tea that had long ago replaced his beer. John answered the telephone, and Alyosha could hear in John's voice that the phone had awoken him. When Kaleena took the phone and asked what was the matter, he could hear that he had awoken her, too.

I just remembered something, Alyosha said.

It's five in the morning.

Five thirty. I waited. I called to apologize. For your rabbit.

Not again with the rabbits.

I didn't know it was yours, Kaleena. I just grabbed one. It was Sunday. Your mama was just in the ground.

What do you mean it was mine?

The orange and white one.

What are you trying to say?

I told you. I want to apologize.

You want to apologize for killing my pet rabbit.

Yes.

You're saying this rabbit is the problem between us.

I remembered it in my dream. What did you call it?

I don't know. I don't care. It was one rabbit.

But it was your pet, Kaleena, and I killed it.

Is this my pet that I used to play with on the grass? On a sunny day, did you say?

Yes, the orange and white one.

What grass, Pop? What grass was there in that dirt lot? Do you mean the thistle? There was plenty of that. Or maybe you're thinking of the burdock.

Cinnamon. You called it Cinnamon.

Do you think you're solving something here? That you found the key, is that it?

I'm admitting it, Kaleena. I'm sorry for it.

Don't you apologize for the rabbits. Don't you fucking do that to me.

But Kaleena—

I killed the rabbits after mama died. You know I did. I fed them and watered them, and every Sunday I took one behind the shed and I killed it for my papa. But you didn't notice. You never noticed.

No. That's not how it was, Alyosha said. But his memory of Kaleena on the grass had become vaporous. He saw a thick stalk of thistle, the pink tuft poking above its spiked bulb.

You didn't see me at all after Mamma died, Kaleena said. You didn't see anything. Everything was behind you.

But, Kaleena. Your mother—

We don't have one rabbit between us. We have a hundred. A hundred dead rabbits. And they didn't have names. Don't come to me with this one rabbit's name.

Kaleena, Alyosha said, I only thought . . . But he had no thought. There was only the dark kitchen around him, his thumb picking at a flake of enamel that had separated from a corner of the table. Then there was Kaleena's sigh reaching him through the telephone.

I have to go, she said. I have to get Molly up. It's done, Pop. We ate the rabbits.

The click of the line disconnecting was quiet, a light tap in Alyosha's ear, and he held his phone there until he heard the dashed tones of a dead line. His tea had cooled, and he placed the unfinished cup into the sink. He opened a cupboard and took down two large bowls, reaching with his left hand, his right shoulder still too sore for the task. Into one bowl he crumbled a length of sausage. I'll have to buy you some proper food, he said. You can't live on sausage. He poured water into the other bowl and carried them both to the front door. He remembered the corpse of the rabbit in his dream, as big as Muffy, lying in the flower bed. Water spilled onto his forearm as he balanced the bowls against his body, and as he pulled on the doorknob, he felt an irrational dread that he would find the rabbit's corpse in the dog's place. But as the door opened, the source of his dread shifted, and he thought to himself, No, not a rabbit's corpse.

He stepped onto the porch and looked down at the flower bed. The sun was not yet up, and he squinted into the darkness. For a moment, he thought he saw the still form of Muffy's body. But as his eyes adjusted, his vision burned through the dog, and he saw that it was not a dog at all, only the hollowed space of the dog's body pressed into the leaves.

He could see where the dog's head had lain, a smaller impression at one tip of the oval bed. He could see where its hind foot had dug into the leaves as the dog dreamed. The longer he looked, the more clearly he saw the dog's contour, an impression so nearly perfect that Muffy seemed almost to be lying there even now. Twice he opened his mouth to speak to the dog, and then he took the rake from where it leaned against the bricks and stroked once over Muffy's bed. His shoulder ached deeply, but even so he set to work raking the flower bed. The sky was clear, and as he looked up, just before dawn, Alyosha could in fact see through the deep blue to the blackness of space beyond.

INSTEAD
OF WHAT WE
COULD HAVE SAID

We lay on our backs, the sheet knotted at our feet, you looking straight ahead, I trying to decide who had been the first not to speak after our failure. From below, the high shouts of children at play drifted through our fourth-floor window like wisps of smoke.

"I think I'll stop by the office today," I finally said. "Just for a few hours."

And you asked, do you remember, "What about the park?"

"Let's not," I told you. I needed you to ask, though. I hoped, even, that you would insist.

Instead, you said, "Yes. Maybe we shouldn't."

My pulse banged in the side of my neck, and I thought, what kind of mother are you? How dare you pretend not to grieve. Monster, I wanted to say. You inhuman monster.

Instead I said, "Maybe I'll spend the whole day at the office."

You said okay, and you stood and put on a bra and underwear. I hated you for that. But what choice did you have? You could have said son of a bitch, but I would only have said what are you talking about. You could have said it's over. You could have said we're dead inside.

You could have told me you see our child every time you look at me. You could have asked how long I left her alone. Instead, you said, "I'll make you some coffee."

Monster.

I'm sure you heard the cleaners dragging the hose up the back steps before I did. You've always been the more perceptive. Even when I said I was going to the office, I knew you read me laid out as plainly as I was laid out naked on the bed beside you, shrinking and defensive.

I followed you into the kitchen, still naked, as if my nakedness might prove that you were the quitter. I was still game. You put too much coffee into the press, and you turned the gas on so high that the flame licked up the handle of the little kettle. The old press had been bigger. The stove had been electric.

Outside the kitchen door, we both heard the thump of the workman's boots and the drag and slap of the empty hose. Can you believe we didn't say a word? Only a month had passed since the first time they'd hosed down the back steps. That time we lay on the bed and held each other as if the building were coming down around us. That time you said, "Let's go to the park and watch the children play," and we grabbed our keys and ran out the front door.

We said it was the only apartment we could find, but we must have thought we deserved it. The day we moved in, it was the super who saw you looking at the darkened window in the kitchen.

"The soot only collects on the back side," he told us as he walked around the four tight rooms flicking light switches. "It's the ash from the cement plant. We hose it down once a month."

I don't know if you heard him. I don't know if reason mattered. You were watching the window as you so often would in the days to come. I put my hand around yours then. I said it would be all right.

This morning, to my shame, I said nothing as the man in his coveralls plodded by the kitchen door and up the final flight of steps. To your shame, you didn't give in to your tears. Do you think about this moment as often as I? We had less than a minute to say or do something, anything. One minute to prove to each other that we were not monsters.

The pump on the water truck started slowly, a countdown—ri ki ta ri ki ta—and I thought I really would grab you. I thought there was enough time, and I was a big enough man. I would grab you and squeeze you again as if the building were coming down around us. But it got fast so quickly—ri ki ta ri ki ta rikita.

I couldn't think.

Even the most awkward word or embrace would have been enough to keep a thread between us, to give us something to work with later, when we were ready to mend. We still could have sprinted out the front door. We could have watched the children in the park. We could have talked about it, and I could have called it *the* lamp by the crib instead of *your* lamp.

Instead, we stood, ridiculous, in the small hot kitchen. Do you remember? You were as frozen as I. You had a carton of milk in your hand. The refrigerator door was open, and I could feel the cold air swirling around my feet.

I don't know if you heard me moan when the hose started. It took the biggest part of me to make even that small sound.

Somehow you managed to close the refrigerator while I stood naked and dull as the water pounded the walls outside. You reached for the kettle just as the water battered the back door. I saw the gas flame wrapped around the kettle's handle, but I didn't think to warn you. I couldn't think at all. When I look back, I can't believe how long you held on. Your elbow knocked over the milk. I remember that. I don't remember if you screamed when you felt the searing hot handle, or if I shouted when the boiling water splashed across my ankles. I don't remember hearing anything until you pulled open the back door.

Water sprayed from the high-pressure hose into the kitchen, and I heard a hollow rumble as it whipped along the wall by my head. I didn't hear your voice until the workman pulled the lever on the hose and the water stopped.

"—away from here!" you yelled. "Where was your water two months ago? Where were you then, you bastard?"

You were soaking wet. The workman was standing in the doorway, and you were beating him on his chest. Your underwear clung translucently to your body, and I remember thinking, my god, she's so beautiful.

Do you remember on our honeymoon, there had been a storm, and we had walked along the beach the next morning? You were already showing then, your stomach another curve I had grown to love. The beach was littered with debris from the storm—seaweed, chunks of coral, old planks of wood. And then we saw a balloon, bright red and still inflated, a bit of streamer trailing off its end. We wondered how it had gotten there, remember? Was it from a birthday party? Was it on a ship that had gone down in the storm? Did people drown while it stayed afloat?

I don't remember how long the workman stared at me before I moved, naked, to grab your wrists. I don't remember us hitting the floor. I don't remember him walking away. I just remember the water and milk pooling around us as we sat shivering on the checkered linoleum.

FLOODPLAIN

1.

We would move to the house by the river in the spring. Karl called it the perfect getaway. He said it was what he needed. Karl always needed something. To be fair, he was under a lot of stress. Up for tenure in one year, dropped by Norton, his department chair not returning his emails.

"Janey, I need this," he said in that wheedling way of his, that coercive use of my name, his tone suggesting that the deal on the house was already done (and it was a lot further along than he'd led me to believe that evening), both of us just waiting for me to come around. He was standing over me as I sat grading papers on the couch. "You can see how much this means to me, Janey," he said, finishing the last sip of his wine. "Can't you?"

He knew I couldn't object on work-related grounds. I could use the seclusion as much as he. I, too, was working on a book. Another composition textbook, my third, and the one for which I was least motivated. The reintroduction of the classic rhetorical modes had been hot the previous two years—so much for Flowers and Elbow and that crew. It's Tea Party time now. Take back Western Civ. I would stand out by out-traditionaling the neo-traditionalists. I would rescue the orphaned child of rhetoric—I would trot out Memory, with a capital M. Mnemonics. Recitation. Classification. Systematization. Brain exercise would be Wadsworth's marketing spin. They already had a webpage—a da Vinci-like drawing of a brain, Latin phrases labeling the lobes, and a quote from Aristotle that I could only think of as ironic for yet another composition textbook: "It is not once nor twice, but times without number that the same ideas make their appearance in the world." I felt the weight of those times without number every time I sat down to write, grains of sand clogging the crevices of my mind.

But unlike Karl, I did write. Two hours a day during the spring, and up to six a day that summer.

"Your problem isn't where you live," I told him. He had moved to the wine rack in the dining room, was reading labels. "Your problem is that you don't do the work."

"Thank you, Janey," he said as he pulled a bottle from the rack. "Thank you for that insightful summation of my 'problem.'"

"You're welcome."

He cut the foil from the neck of the bottle and unscrewed the cork, his elbow flapping with the twisting of the screw. He was going to be dramatic.

"Janey," he said, holding the bottle high over the glass as he poured. "For the last five years—" He set the bottle down, ran his finger up the side to catch a drip, licked his finger. "For the last five years, I've sat on committees, agreeing with strategic plans made by people who couldn't find their way around the campus where they've worked since the Nixon admin-istration. I've had to kiss the asses of people so old they shit dust. In those five years I stood up once and said no. One time. You know what happened?"

"Norton dropped you."

"Norton dropped me. Thanks again for your insight, Janey."

"You stood up to the wrong people, Karl. You were supposed to stand up to the people who shit dust, not the people who shit money."

"So here I am, six months away from losing my job, from losing my career, Janey. Losing my career. And now I've found this house. This house that no one wanted. That no one even knew existed. This house where I can have solitude. Time to write."

He was walking toward me, his wine glass waving with the cadence of his voice, keeping time like a conductor's baton. He had spent the first bottle of wine telling me about the house. How it was right under those assholes' noses, but they couldn't see it. "Assholes' noses?" I had asked, but he hadn't let it get to him.

The house was in the floodplain, in a neighborhood that the city had moved to demolish. Three of the last five years had seen record "hundred-year" floods, and the city had passed a motion to buy up a pocket of properties in twelve square blocks that lay below the sixty-one-foot mark. They would demolish the houses and turn the area into green space. Karl had first heard at the bar about the sixty-two-foot house that sat on the riverbank, surrounded by that sixty-one-foot neighborhood. The city hadn't realized the situation until the legislation had already been passed, "sixty-one feet" scattered throughout hundreds of pages of documents, signatures of approval inked by politicians all the way up to the state capital. It was a done deal. The house was an orphan.

Karl showed me the spot on a contour map, the brown horseshoe line that pulled away from the river's bank and rejoined it a mile to the south. "That line marks sixty-one feet," he'd said. "Inside that line is the neighborhood." Then he showed me a small, irregular brown circle, like a deflated balloon lying on the riverbank, in the center of the horseshoe. "That's sixty-two feet," he said. "And in the middle of that circle is our house."

He had called the owner when he'd come home from the bar, the same night he'd heard about the house. The man lived in Arizona, had been renting the place out, but was between tenants, and he and Karl both knew he would never get another tenant. Karl had made a lowball offer that same night over the phone. The man had accepted. What could he do? Fight city hall? From Arizona?

"Just give me this one thing," Karl said to me as he sat beside me on the couch. "Give *us* this one thing, Janey." His chin dipped to his chest, and he aimed his furrowed brow at me, his pouted lips. Back to humble now. I imagined being his colleague—we both taught English, but at different schools, he at the state school, I at a liberal arts college—imagined watching this puddling of a man in the middle of the day, at a conference table under the glare of fluorescent lights. It was painful enough to watch here, in the evening, in lamplight after a glass of wine.

As repelled as I was by Karl at that moment, however, I was still intrigued by the idea of the house. As I said, I, too, thought I could use the solitude. I'd never fully understood Karl's procrastination with his book until I'd started this latest composition project. My writing sessions had become torturous, hair-pulling hours of verbal self-flagellation. I would rather be doing anything, and though I hardly admitted it to myself, I had begun to spend much of my time posting replies on forums for people looking for grammar and language help. My favorite site was grammargirl.com. Kids asked when to use "whose" versus "who's," and wondered what split infinitives are and why they aren't supposed to be split. My first step toward my career as a rhetorician had been tutoring classmates in high school, and in college I had worked in the writing center. Okay, I had lived in the writing center. Now I lived in my office, lived in front of my computer. Of the four classes I taught each year, only one was a writing class, the others pedagogy and theory. When a boy posted a question asking why "attorneys general" wasn't "attorney generals," I jumped for my mouse.

I was also intrigued by how Karl got the house—how he just took it. I was reminded of when we'd first met. We were in graduate school, at a party thrown by a professor and her husband. Karl was the one in the corduroy jacket. The one standing in the professors' circle, holding a scotch on the rocks and laughing louder than everyone around him. Anyone could see how silly he was, with his leather patches on his elbows and his hand sweeping back that thick tangle of brown bangs as he quoted Alexander Pope and Oscar Wilde. This, when he was offered another drink: "I can resist anything but temptation!" Anyone could see how silly he was, but he had such conviction. The circle of people around him grew. I was across the room, somehow always standing between groups, telling myself not to drink so fast but needing to look occupied. We made eye contact, and he winked at me as if he had been sure I would look up just then. "Don't move," his wink had said. "I'll be right there." As if we were already acquainted, already lovers. As if that night in his bed beneath the Henry James poster were already a foregone conclusion.

But something about those four years of graduate school changed him. He'd struggled for an extra three semesters on his dissertation, an examination of silences in Elizabethan literature, and then only just squeaked past his defense. I once asked why he'd chosen the topic. I hadn't known him to be silent. Ever. "I don't really remember," he said. He supposed he'd thought it would be easy. For five years since, he'd sat on the book he'd begun, pulling it out with a big production every six or eight months, working with a flourish for a few weeks after Norton offered him the contract. "I took a wrong turn," he said the night Norton dropped him, as he lay drunk on the floor. "I just don't know where."

For a moment, when he broke the news of the house in the floodplain, I saw that winking boy in the corduroy jacket. I remembered the pressure of his hand, spread across my sternum as it had been that night under the gaze of Henry James. But just as quickly, the boy was gone, the pressure of Karl's hand giving way to the pressure of his sales pitch.

He set his glass of wine on the end table and placed his hand on my knee. I was wearing shorts, and his fingers moved up my thigh. Still the furrowed brow, the pouted lips, his thickening voice, burbling like an infant. "Baby, it could be so good in that house," he said. His hand slid farther up my thigh. He nuzzled his head into my shoulder. I knew he was getting an erection. We'd been through this routine so many times, his coming up to me as if I were his mother and he had just skinned his knee. But all hands and hard-on, too. Put yourself in my place, women of the world. Put yourself there on that couch with him wallowing in his self-pity as he ferrets his way up the leg of your shorts hoping for a hand job. That's what our lovemaking had become. This was our marriage.

"Fine," I said. "Just get off me." He pulled away, injured. "Oh, please," I said. "I agreed, okay. We'll go."

He waited for me to recant, and when I didn't he kissed me hard on the lips. "You won't regret this," he said. I listened for the dramatic punctuation of my name, but to my surprise it didn't come.

We moved in on the first Saturday after the school year ended. The last resident had moved out of the neighborhood a week earlier, and Karl drove the U-Haul over the curb to get around the construction barrier that blocked the road. The ground was still half-covered in snow, left over from a freak late-April storm that dumped eighteen inches, and the crusted bank scraped the underside of the truck. I heard something crash as we dropped back into the street. "That was the china cabinet," I said. "I told you we should have tied it down."

It was dusk, and the houses were dark—black rectangles of windows against moon-white clapboard and stucco, the low profiles of bungalows and, here and there, a tall Victorian or Gothic revival. A plastic dump truck lay on its side in front of one of the Victorians, a child's shovel stuck in a patch of snow beside it. Newly sprouted daffodils rose from the melting flower bed near the open front door, and, as I watched, something hairy and humped leapt from the flower bed and slipped into the house.

"Jesus," I said. "Did you see that? What was that?"

The streetlights flickered on. "I wonder when they'll cut the power," Karl said.

"Cut the power? What about us?"

"We'll be okay. I talked with the utility company. We may lose power for a while if we flood, but they're leaving our lines live. We'll get a propane tank for gas. Water and sewer will stay. They'll be putting in public bathrooms for the park eventually, so they'll need the infrastructure."

"When will they start tearing down the houses?"

"I don't know. Not for a while. Not until the snow melts and they see what the river will do. Not until the ground dries up later this summer." Karl propped his forearm on the steering wheel and pointed straight ahead. "There she is."

Our house wasn't like the other houses in the neighborhood. It was a farmhouse that the neighborhood had grown up around, the original owners having parceled out their field and sold it in lots a hundred years ago, creating the neighborhood.

I had visited the house before we signed the papers, but it looked different now, at night, without the full blanket of snow. It sat back, away from the road, the front yard filled with trees, bare branches lacing the tall white peak of its roof. Behind it was the darkness of thickening woods, cedar and hemlock that sloped down the riverbank.

When I stepped from the truck I could hear the river. It sounded deeper than I had remembered. Or wider. It hardly sounded at all, really, and I thought I felt it more than heard it, a low pitch that resonated through my feet. "This place gives me the creeps," I said. Karl was looking into the darkness toward the sound of the river, inhaling, an idiotic smile on his face. "You look like you're eight years old," I told him.

"I feel like it," he said.

We spent that first night camped in sleeping bags on the living-room floor. There was a wood stove but no wood, and after we fell asleep we moved closer to one another, unconsciously searching for a little bit of extra warmth. At some point in the night we were kissing. We didn't make love, but Karl reached into my sleeping bag and held me until we drifted back to sleep.

The next morning, the sky was gloomy as we unloaded the truck, and after a lunch of tuna-fish sandwiches we returned the U-Haul. The sky had been dark all day, and as we drove our car back into the neighborhood, rain began to fall.

It didn't let up for three days.

I spent that time setting up my office in the back bedroom upstairs. Karl spent it draped in wires. First there was the stereo. Then the home theater. Then the internet. He fished wires through walls, stapled them along baseboards, twisted them into the backs of speakers, plugged them into routers.

"Maybe you should rethink your line of work," I told him one day. I was taking a break from writing and had just put a kettle on the stove. Karl was on a ladder, pushing into the ceiling a coat hanger to which he had taped a long gray cable.

"I have to be able to get online," he said. "We should be good to go tomorrow."

But something went wrong with the installation, and Karl spent another two days rechecking wires, typing names, passwords, and strings of numbers into the computer before he finally gave up.

The next morning, as I wrote in my office behind my closed door, I heard Karl going up and down the stairs, into and out of the room adjacent to mine, a third bedroom that was to be Karl's office. His work lay on the floor in cardboard boxes labeled "Karl's Work," the boxes still sealed with packing tape.

I heard a hammer pound a nail into the wall that separated us. Then, for the rest of the morning, I heard the thunk of darts hitting his dartboard. I was sure he'd intentionally hung the board on the wall between us, and for the first half hour I jumped at each plunk of the darts. But as they continued, I began to feel comforted by them, empowered. With each set of three, I was sure Karl was telling himself "Just one more set and I'll start to work." Just one more, and one more, and one more. I had known that he didn't get much done at his office at school, but I hadn't been there to see him avoid the work. Somehow having it happen right here in front of me was motivating. I almost dreaded his starting to write, as if I might have to subtract his daily page count from my own. The sentences flowed across my screen, one more, and one more, and one more, the plunk of darts marking time. My fingers grew cramped, and I massaged them, the stiff pain a red badge of courage.

I froze when I heard the static of tape being torn from the cardboard boxes. I strained my ears to hear the sound of his keyboard, unsure whether the chiclet hum would travel through the wall. I tried to remember

168   VINCENT REUSCH

where I'd been, something about topic sentences. Transitions? Damn him. Was he writing? I walked across the room, pressed my ear against the wall. Nothing. He would be reading first, trying to get back into his work—massaging its heart, giving it mouth-to-mouth. I couldn't imagine trying to bring that tired old carcass back to life. Again. That poor thing. Let it rest in peace. I sat back at my keyboard, but all I could think of was Karl sorting his thoughts, sketching a thumbnail outline. I wanted the rhythm of those darts, that slow heartbeat, that gasping breath.

Then I heard Karl's door open, his feet pound down the steps. I heard the stretch of the spring on the back door, the slap of the wooden frame as he stepped outside. I added another sentence. It was a bad one, a hitch somewhere in the syntax—a "to which" and a "so that" duking it out in the same sentence—but I didn't care. There it was, line upon line, page upon page, another project inching toward completion.

Three more days passed. I wrote my six hours each day. Karl moved from his dartboard, back to his struggle with the internet connection (again to no avail), to a chaise lounge that he had found in our garden shed and placed in the backyard facing the river. Then one morning, the chair was in the river, the water having crested the bank and crawled halfway up our back lawn.

The rise in the river wasn't only due to the rain we'd just had, but to the whole winter's worth of snow, melted and percolated into the soil, leaching beneath thousands of acres of farmers' fields, moving inexorably toward the river.

Each morning, I listened to the forecast on the radio. At fifty-seven feet, the city built clay dikes around our neighborhood, sealing us in. At fifty-eight feet, Karl came home with a little red wagon that he'd found in someone's garage. We strapped on backpacks, climbed over the dikes, and pulled the wagon to a nearby grocery store to stock up on canned and dry goods. At fifty-nine feet, Karl gathered firewood from a neighbor's woodpile and stacked it against the back of our house. At sixty, our power went out. Then, the next morning, the river reached sixty-one feet and crept without a sound into the neighborhood.

The streets filled first, water reaching along them like fingers before it crept over the curbs and fanned across lawns. It poured through basement windows and rose up between floorboards, lifted the dolls and dust mops and stained throw pillows that had been left behind, pooled around abandoned beds and couches.

It crested at sixty-two feet, leaving Karl and me stranded in the middle of that deflated balloon I'd seen on the map.

2.

I wrote longhand on the first day of the flood, not wanting to break my routine, despite the power outage. I wondered what Karl would do. He couldn't play with his wires without power. And even he couldn't spend entire days playing darts. With trepidation, I thought that he would now have no choice but to work on his book.

I didn't know about the rowboat tied to the railing by the back door. I heard the splash of the oars and looked out my window in time to see him round the corner of the house.

When he returned just before sunset, his boat was filled with books. "They left their entire library," he said as he unloaded the boat and stacked the books in the living room, "dry as a bone on the second floor."

"You went into someone's house?" I asked.

"I went into no one's house," he said.

For the next two days, Karl went on his odysseys, returning with hand tools, fishing tackle, a collection of old postcards that he couldn't believe anyone would leave behind. "I need your help," he said when he returned empty-handed on that second afternoon. "I can't get it into the boat alone."

He wouldn't say what "it" was. He had rubber boots waiting for me by the door. I don't know where he got them. "I'm writing," I told him as I pushed my feet into the boots—they were a perfect fit. I hadn't been writing, though. I had spent the morning watching a refrigerator float almost imperceptibly slowly out of the neighborhood until it disappeared behind the half-submerged trees that had once marked the riverbank.

Karl sat backward in the bow of the boat and rowed us for several blocks. He tied up at the front porch of a tall yellow house, and we slogged through the water that covered the first floor nearly to the height of our boots. The house was dark, the sun just setting outside. I followed Karl upstairs to the half-emptied library. "Isn't it great?" he asked.

It was a Victrola. He opened its front and inside were several dozen records. We carried it out, and I steadied the boat while Karl stood the player in the stern. He cranked the handle and put on a record. The Victrola cleared its throat with a few hisses and pops, and then the pinched sound of an orchestra began, a tenor opening up, fuller than I thought possible from the old machine, the voice skipping like a stone across the flat water.

"Who is it?" I asked.

"Giovanni Martinelli, performing '*Torna a Surriento.*'" he said.

I sat on the floor, in the space between Karl's legs, and he rowed as Martinelli sang.

That night, we lit candles and drank wine together in the living room as the Victrola played Stravinsky and Mahler, Glenn Miller and Benny Goodman, tunes from *Porgy and Bess* and *Show Boat*. Moonlight shimmered on the ceiling, reflected off the river that lay, as if listening, two feet from our windows.

We made love on the floor that night, our sex a mutual coming-together, Karl's approach direct and presumptive, so unlike those sneaking fingers and averted eyes that I'd grown used to. We fell asleep as soon as we'd finished and awoke in the morning having hardly moved.

The river stayed high—the neighborhood flooded, the power out—for three weeks. I wrote longhand in my office in the mornings for a few more days after our trip in the rowboat, wrote each day until Karl returned from his morning excursions and lured me downstairs with the scent of B&M baked beans, Dinty Moore beef stew, or Campbell's tomato soup, our lunch heating on the cast-iron top of the wood stove.

In the evenings, we took turns reading selections from the new books while we sat by the open door of the wood stove. The books were mostly classics, matching collections of blue- or red-cloth hardcovers. Something about the isolation, the lack of electricity, the air of tragedy as the river rose around us, steered us toward the Russians—Dostoevsky, Gogol, Tolstoy—Raskolnikov's panicked voice reverberating through Karl's body as my head rested in his lap.

After reading, we would play the Victrola and lie in the heat of the wood stove, naked in each other's arms. Each night we stayed up a little later, and each morning my writing sessions grew shorter as I awoke at eight and then nine and then ten, Karl up and gone in the boat long before I opened my eyes.

By the end of the week I was lying in bed almost until he returned, not wanting to write, not wanting to be alone in the house without him. I wanted him in the living room with me, on the floor in the light of a kerosene lantern (another neighborhood find), the books scattered around us.

I was watching Karl shave one night when I asked him where he went in the boat.

"Just around," he said.

He had heated a pan of water on the wood stove and was shaving by candlelight. I had taken some of the water for coffee, and I poured into the coffee a slow drizzle of sweetened condensed milk. "Around where?" I asked.

"The neighborhood," he said. He'd acquired a straight razor, brush, and soap from one of the vacant houses, and as he wet and lathered his five-day beard I watched the brush paint across the curve of his raised jaw, up the knot of his Adam's apple.

"What do you do?" I asked. I sipped the coffee, and the condensed milk coated my lips.

"I rescued a cat this morning," he said. "It was up a tree. I rowed it to the dike."

He held a rectangular piece of glass, a scouting mirror, I thought, and I imagined him finding it in a treehouse with the stranded cat, imagined his boat tied to the wooden rungs that ran in a crooked line up the tree's trunk, Karl pulling himself easily up into the canopy, the cat in a corner, shaking and hungry.

"It would have starved," I said.

Karl nodded, his head tipped to one side. He raised the straight razor to his face, and it flashed red in the light from the open wood stove.

I licked my lips, the coffee and the sweetened milk combining to taste like chocolate. "I want to go with you," I said.

"What about your writing? Your page count?"

"You know I don't do a page count."

"How about your hours?" he asked.

I could hear the scrape as he ran the razor up his cheek, the skin behind the fire-lit blade wiped clean. When he saw that I was watching, he winked at me, the same wink I remembered from so long ago. He swirled the blade in the pan of hot water, and the soft scent of shaving cream rose with the steam.

"To hell with my hours," I said.

The sky was filled with low clouds as we rowed away from the house the next morning, cracks between them letting through angled shafts of sunlight. Showers fell here and there, dark smudges that crawled around the floodplain. Karl rowed us along the avenues, between columns of flooded houses, to the edge of the neighborhood where the

VINCENT REUSCH

dike rose from the water. We sat low in the boat, and the clay dike towered over us so that we could see only sky above it.

"It looks like the end of the world," I said.

"The end of our world," Karl said. He rotated one oar in circles, and we turned back toward the neighborhood. He was wearing cutoff jean shorts and leather sandals, no shirt, and I watched the muscles rise in his shoulders as he rowed.

"How many houses have you been into?" I asked.

"A few dozen," he said.

"How do you choose which ones to go into?"

"Which one do you want to go into?"

I pointed to a craftsman with a large front porch whose floor sat above the water. "Let's go there," I said.

We docked the boat at the foot of the porch steps. The front door was unlocked, and we stepped inside.

"It's beautiful," I said. The floors were wood, the trim dark and heavy. The sound of water lapping at the base of the house echoed around the rooms. "I feel like I'm underwater."

We went upstairs and found that the bed had been left in the master bedroom.

"It's king size," Karl said. "They didn't want to deal with getting it out. You'd be surprised how many people leave their beds."

I ran my hand down his smooth, bare chest. "It would be a shame to let it go to waste," I said.

He put his arm around me. I was wearing a cotton summer dress, and I could feel through the thin fabric each finger as he ran his hand down to the small of my back. He pulled me into himself, and we fell together onto the mattress.

His stomach was firm beneath mine. "You're losing weight," I said.

"No beer," he said. He pulled up my dress, and the cool cotton rose up the backs of my legs.

We made love on the bare mattress, the ghostly chime of waves reverberating through the walls around us.

That was when I quit writing.

For the first few days, the decision not to write came consciously. I deserve a break, I told myself. This is a special time. This flooded neighborhood will never be again. I'd be a fool not to take advantage of it.

But there was also the allure of Karl. We spent our mornings exploring in the rowboat, our afternoons making love in empty houses, our evenings making love in front of the wood stove. Our sex evolved during the flood, from tender reacquaintance to excited exploration to fearlessness, shamelessness. We took from each other, gave to each other, forgot anything of a bashful glance. I was gone, I realized one night as we made love. "The Rite of Spring" had just finished playing on the Victrola, the orchestra climaxing before us, and we continued in time to the stylus that popped, regular as a heartbeat, against the edge of the paper label. I had never felt so lost in anything, had never known how liberating getting lost could be.

3.

When the river receded, the neighborhood as we had known it was gone. Silt covered everything, a reddish brown membrane that obscured the streets and flattened the shrubs. Deadfall lay everywhere, mud-encased trees lying crushed on their sides. The power returned, though no utility workers came to the house.

In the first days after the flood, we tried to explore the neighborhood on foot, but the silt was slick and dangerous to walk on. The houses we entered stank now of stagnant water and mildew, dead fish drying on the floors. The evenings at home were no longer the same, either. The nights were too warm now for a fire, and instead of camping in front of the wood stove, we sat on upholstered furniture, across the room from each other. I missed the uneven planks of the floor against my hips, missed lying fitted into the crevices of Karl's body.

Our lovemaking also changed. In the glare of electric lights our abandon felt shameful. We turned off the lights, but our timidity had left us shaken, and our sex became a lurching, halting affair that ended one night in failure. Afterwards, as Karl sat on the floor with his knees pulled to his chest, I could feel the distance between us, expanding with the receding water, our balloon stretching, the strain palpable.

The day after our failure, Karl took a rake into the backyard, and for the first time in two weeks I returned to my office. My papers lay where I had left them, my work looking now like a museum exhibit, something that should be kept behind glass, cordoned off by velvet ropes. Come see where Jane Wallace did her final work, her home office preserved for posterity.

Only for what posterity? For whom to remember? My only readers were college freshmen forced to buy my textbooks, and Wadsworth intentionally ran the books out of print every two years in order to defeat the used-book market.

I spent two days finding my way back into the work, poring over passages, reconstructing the logic that connected one chapter with the next. I reread dozens of pages, skimmed a hundred or more—thousands upon thousands of words, each feeling so heavy, the sum of their weight incalculable. I worked in spurts, paced the room, stood at the window for half an hour at a time, watching Karl, who spent those days reopening the sloping lawn as the floodwaters eased their way back into their banks. He worked shirtless in his cutoff jean shorts and brown leather sandals, his back and arms tanned now to the color of the mud around him. He carried loads of branches down to the river, raked and shoveled silt, piled the drowned carcasses of mice and squirrels into a bucket, and buried them on the riverbank.

I was at the window, thinking of another term for "compare and contrast," something with more Google-age appeal—X vs. Y, Apples to Windows, C&C—when I saw a rabbit eating from Karl's hand. Karl was holding the fat end of something that resembled a small white carrot, while the rabbit held the thin end in its paws and nibbled on the tip. "It was a Queen Anne's lace," Karl told me when he came in that evening. "It's in the carrot family."

He knew about the Queen Anne's lace because he'd read about it. He'd found among the books he'd gathered a collection of field guides—plants, birds, mammals, tracking—and he read them from cover to cover as I finished *Anna Karenina* on my own.

The rabbit was followed by more rabbits, hopping around our yard and following Karl as he hauled wagons filled with weeds from an old plot of garden he'd discovered. More came, and they fanned their territory into the empty neighborhood. Coyotes followed the rabbits, and at night we would listen through the open window to their bawling. All at once, they would cry like babies. "They're on the hunt," Karl would say, and a moment later the terrified squeal of a rabbit would shock the night. Then the raccoons came, their humped backs in the darkness, waddling across the dirt-filled streets. Then the deer moved in, grazing from feral gardens in the mornings, bedding down with the sunset in the grass that had begun to grow so fast through the rich deposits of silt. Turkeys pecked by in flocks. Beavers smacked their tails on the river's smooth surface, breaking the water into a crystalline spray. Turtles sunned themselves in driveways. Eagles nested in the dead limbs of a diseased elm in view of our bedroom window. I fretted for hours each day at my keyboard. Karl grew a beard.

As June wore on, Karl began increasingly to stay away from home in the evenings. I would go to bed alone, and sometime in the night he would slip into bed beside me, bringing with him the cool scent of the night air.

When he did stay in and read with me, he seemed unable to concentrate on his book. One evening, I peered over the top of my page and watched him as he sat reading in a rocking chair on the far side of the room. He was shirtless, hunched over his book, which looked small and fragile in his callused hands, as if the book were one of the birds or wildflowers he was reading about, as if it were an animal track at the edge of the river, delicate and fleeting. His knee bounced. The chair fidgeted more than rocked. Soon, I reassured myself, he would be back to his wiring. Back to his four glasses of wine every night. Back to his grandstanding and pettiness and servility, to all those things that accompany and propagate the deflection of his failure.

He saw me watching him, and he started in with some did-you-knows about animals. As in, "Did you know that a mole can dig three hundred feet in one night?" Or, "Did you know that a cockroach can survive for two weeks without a head? That it will die of starvation?"

"Did you know," I asked, "that you haven't written a single word all summer?"

"Did you know," he asked, "that a snail can sleep for three years?"

"Did you know that you're going to lose your tenure bid this fall?"

"Did you know," he asked, "that an ostrich's brain is smaller than its eye?"

"Did you know that I'm not going to support you while you spend your nights rationalizing your failure to your drunk buddies at the bar?"

"Did you know," he asked, "that the female human is the only female of any species known to actively denigrate her own mate?"

"You do a fine job of that without any help from me, Karl."

"And how about you? Do you do a fine job with your life without any help from me?"

"What do you mean?"

"You hate what you do."

"What are you talking about?"

"And you love it when I'm on the ropes."

"Okay. Here we go. The drama. Let's have it, Karl. I've missed it."

"I know you have," he said. "That's what's so sad."

He stood and walked from the room. I heard the

spring and slap of the screen door, and the first burst of his bare feet against the grass as he ran into the darkness.

He didn't come home that night, and I lay awake wondering if he were sleeping in one of the beds where we'd made love. Wondering if he would avoid them. During a break in my writing the next morning, I saw him from my window, standing motionless on the river-bank. Still, he didn't come home the next night, or the next, or the night after that.

4.

Weeks passed. June gave way to July. I wrote. Karl was gone from our house, but not gone from the neighborhood, not gone from what I had begun to think of as his domain. I watched him drag a pile of branches here, wheelbarrow some dirt there. Why? I would never know—we weren't speaking. I saw him most often by the river, looking out over the water, always in his stretched and soiled jean shorts—he had abandoned his sandals, never wore a shirt. He seemed to be waiting, though for what, I was not sure. His beard grew full, his hair wind-tangled. I saw him one evening strip off his shorts and dive without a splash into the river. I waited for him to surface, but he must have slid with the current out of sight, his shorts lying forgotten in the mud.

For a time, I wondered what he was eating, but then I found, on an afternoon walk, a snare trap, set on the riverbank near a network of rabbit tracks. Another time, I saw rising on the wind the downy tufts of feathers, and I traced them back to a bloody patch of ground where I found the head and feet of a turkey. "Have fun, Daniel

Boone," I said to the blank, staring eye of the turkey. A brain no larger than your eye, I thought. Have your fun while it lasts.

Meanwhile, I had been eating from our stockpile of canned goods, and with only a few days' worth left, I steeled myself to go to the grocery store. I didn't want to go, in part because it had been so long since I'd talked to anyone, so long since I'd left the neighborhood, or even thought of life beyond the dikes. But I hesitated, too, because my writing had been going well again. I had set for myself a rigid routine—up at seven, four hours at the keyboard, lunch and a proofread of my morning's work, and then four more hours of writing. Then a long walk through the neighborhood as I outlined my next day's work. I thought about sacrificing a walk for the trip to the store, but aside from contemplation of the book, I truly enjoyed these walks. Karl had been right about the beauty of living alone here. Spring flowers had given way to lush green grasses grown now to waist height, a prairie that had moved in like a tide, houses like ships at anchor. Summer was fat and full, with no hint that fall would ever arrive. Leaving the floodplain at that time seemed almost impossible.

Then one morning I discovered that I wouldn't have to leave, not for food. I found a cookbook on the floor just inside the back door—*How to Serve Wild Game*. I opened the door and found on the step, wrapped in fern fronds, a field-dressed rabbit. I discovered, too, that the garden had been tended all these weeks, and that the carrots and radishes were ripe, spinach and arugula ready to be picked. I cooked a rabbit stew on the wood stove that evening, and for the first time in weeks I remembered, viscerally, Karl's body, warm from the fire.

I drank a bottle of wine as I ate, and when I'd finished it, I opened another.

The second bottle was half-empty on the nightstand as I drifted to sleep. The last thing I remember was feeling with my tongue the slick grease of rabbit still on my lips, tasting the rich pungency of wild game.

I don't know what time Karl came into the bedroom. I awoke to the chuffing of his breath and found him standing naked by the bed.

The scent of the river filled the room. He pressed his face into my neck, his beard wet, his back damp as I wrapped my arms around him. He kissed his way down my stomach, or bit his way, or chewed or licked, his hands clamped at my hips. For an hour I was lost, struggling with him, struggling against him, overwhelmed by his touch, by the thick, night air that seemed to envelop him. I glanced at his face as we came, though I told myself that I wouldn't make this intimate, that he didn't deserve intimacy, that I didn't want it. Moonlight fell from the window across his face, and I saw in his eyes only the paleness and distance of that moon.

I woke the next morning wondering in my half-sleep if his visit had been a dream. If he had been a demon. An angel? But there was the proof: my skin prickling and red, fetid mud drying on the white sheets.

My head throbbed from the wine, but I wrote that day. And the next, and the next, my book moving on from "Cause and Effect" to "Process" to "Report."

Three days later, I once again woke in the night to the animal sounds of his breathing, the scent of the river once again filling the room. Again we made love, or had sex. Whatever you want to call it. I suppose we were fucking. Fucking like animals. I hated him for coming to me like that. I hated him for leaving before morning. I waited eagerly for his return, and I hated myself for that.

And so passed July, with some new wild game showing up on the doorstep every day or two—fish or rabbit or turkey—Karl showing up in my bedroom every third or fourth night. Each time, he was washed in the river, both of us impatient, brutish.

I would still see him occasionally in the distance during my walks, the stringy rag that was left of his shorts slung around his hips, his hair and beard matting into dreadlocks. But only twice did I see him at night, outside the bedroom. The first time, I was at the window. The crying of the coyotes had awoken me, and I looked out just as a rabbit broke from the woods. A second later the pack of coyotes followed. And running with them was Karl, lithe and naked, his long legs pulling one stride for every four of the ribbed, low-slung coyotes.

The second time I saw him I was by the river. The wind had picked up, and I was listening to distant rumbles of thunder, feeling the electric approach of a storm. I was wondering where he stayed. Surely in a house, I thought, and as I wondered which one he would choose, a bolt of lightning struck nearby. In its light, I saw him. He was pulling himself from the river near the opposite shore, climbing an overhanging branch. The flash fixed him in all his detail—the Michaelangelian form that had become his body, the sluicing water frozen in the moment, lightning-sparkled as it fell from the stone of his triceps. In the aftermath of the strike, I was blinded. Thunder echoed down the corridor of river, banging its way from bend to bend, the image of Karl in my mind reverberating with it, crashing and bumping through parts of myself of which I had so little knowledge, so little control. I despised his escape. I envied his freedom. I resented his assurance in the bedroom. And I craved his body.

As my eyesight returned, I saw the pale ghost of him disappear into the canopy of trees, and I thought how hopeless this was for him, how hopeless for me.

With August came a whiff of fall. I smelled it one cool morning. A dryness, a crispness, something papery. The day was breezy, and the leaves rattled more loudly than I had noticed before. There was a feeling of electricity in the air, an electric blue in the sky, a seasonal shift in the flat-bottomed cumulus clouds that drifted overhead. All day, I felt uneasy.

That night the breeze continued to play through the dry treetops, and a full moon broke at intervals from behind the passing clouds as I looked out the window, hoping for a glimpse of Karl, who hadn't visited for almost two weeks. When I saw him crouched on the ridgeline of the tallest house in the neighborhood, I was sure he had been there, unmoving, the entire time I had been at the window. He was thinner than I'd remembered, his skin alabaster in the light of the full moon. He was facing away from me, away from the river, intent upon something on the horizon, where our wilderness met the world. I watched him for half an hour as he remained motionless on that roof. My head nodded, heavy with sleep, and when I looked again he was gone.

5.

I didn't understand the sound that woke me the next morning. For months, I had heard only the wind in the trees, the hum of the river. I didn't understand the grating, the snapping, the huffing chug of diesel. I didn't understand, afraid for my life as the floor vibrated beneath me in time with the distant, but ever so powerful, crunch and slap. I didn't understand anything until one seismic shudder brought clarity, something in the sound of demolition unmistakable, though I had never before heard a house being torn down.

My book was just days from completion. I was finishing the research paper section and would then cut and paste the grammar-and-style handbook. I thought of Karl, frozen on the rooftop, his play cut short by the ruination of his territory, and I went to my office to write, sure that the sound of demolition would be as motivating as the thunk of darts. It wasn't. And for the first time in more than a month, I stopped my writing an hour early.

As I walked toward the edge of the neighborhood, several deer bounded past me, running toward the river. A panicked rabbit bumped into my leg.

Closer to the demolition, I realized that the sound was not of a single vehicle destroying a single home, but of dozens of vehicles, dozens of homes. The machines had set up a picket line, had rolled together over the dike, and were tearing away at the perimeter of the floodplain.

Excavators moved in clumsy syncopation. As they raised their greasy necks and brought their rusted buckets down on the houses, I was reminded of something I might see in a child's picture book. The buckets were toothed, with hinged lids that worked like jaws, and they bit into the houses and spit brick and shingles and splintered wood into the dump trucks that sat near their iron-clad treads. One worked as a battering ram, curling its bucket down and pushing to topple chimneys and uproot hundred-year-old trees. It nudged with comic gentleness on the face of a house that looked whole, but proved, as it fell, to be only a gruesome mask, the house gutted already from behind by another excavator. As that last remaining wall floated to the ground, I thought it seemed surprised. I had seen the same stunned disbelief earlier that summer, on the face of a fish that looked up at me from just beneath the surface of the silted river. It had looked at me only for a moment before its eyes glassed over and it rolled to reveal the jutting spike of its severed spine, a few ribbons of flesh, its body taken a second earlier by a snapping turtle.

The iron jaws of the excavators dove again and again into roofless houses, resurfacing with mouths full of drywall and kitchen cupboards, refrigerators and six-panel doors, two-by-fours poking like toothpicks from their corrugated teeth. I was two houses away from the nearest and could hear the snap of individual studs. I watched it dive deep into the house and resurface with a clawfoot bathtub dangling by a length of iron pipe. The tub was enameled white, its stubby feet intricately carved—embarrassingly so—a source of vanity that had remained secret beneath the tub's corpulent body, now held aloft like a joke for the amusement of the other excavators.

I turned away and ran back to the house.

When the machines stopped at the end of the day, the rabbits crept from the underbrush. The deer rose from the grasses, stunned and skittish.

I slept fitfully that night and awoke before dawn. I went to the window and found Karl standing in the garden, a marble statue, moonlight casting shadows on the undersides of his ribs. The coyotes paced around him, glanced up to his veiled eyes, and scrapped with each other when he offered no solace. A few deer standing close to the river scuffed the ground with their hooves, tipped back their heads, and blew airy, fluting breaths. Karl walked out of the yard, and the animals scattered. All up and down the river that night I heard the coyotes fighting, heard the rabbits squealing, their shrieks like points of light in the darkness.

All the next day, the sound of engines and splintering wood drifted high over the floodplain. And all that day, to my credit or to my shame, I worked on my textbook. For a week the demolition continued, the phalanx closing in by two or three rows of houses each day. And each day my work reached nearer its end.

Then the excavators were close enough for me to see from my upstairs bedroom window the orange humped necks of these deformed giraffes, bobbing above the treetops. Mingled with the smell of grease and diesel and lumber, the lean scent of autumn was now constant. Here and there, the branch of a maple had turned crimson, a cottonwood golden. The prairie around us had browned, grasses gone to seed. Along the river, the bracken ferns began to die, their fronds blackening, tips curling in upon themselves as if in a hopeless attempt to return to the fiddleheads of their birth.

The ground shook as the excavators tore away the last houses around ours. When they finally fell silent, their crooked necks looming in the darkness just outside our home, my book was finished.

That night, I walked past the line of machines, tiptoed around dump trucks and bulldozers, slipped between clay-encrusted iron treads. Beyond that front line, the neighborhood was gone, the land treeless, black, and torn. The air was damp, and fog pooled in the low places, piles of deadfall scattered here and there like barbed wire thickets. Something metallic clicked somewhere deep inside one of the machines, and I ran back to the house.

I awoke again in the middle of the night and found Karl standing naked over our bed. But this time the smell of the river was not on him, his dry and catching breath not the animal chuff I was used to. I studied the jut of his collar bones, the protruding crests of his thin hips. He lay beside me, curled his cold porcelain body inward, and I ran my hand along the jagged contour of his shoulder, pushed my fingers into his tangled hair.

He cried, and I heard in his voice the fluting of the deer, the baying of the coyotes. Then there was no sound, his mouth open in a silent wail, and I thought of the river, of those thousands of gallons of water that flowed so quietly past our house each day, so easy to dismiss until they broke from their banks and flooded the plain. How astonishing, I thought, that the water can ever again fit into the confines of those banks, the genie retreat back into its bottle. How astonishing that we would go back to school. That Karl would put together the packet for his failed tenure bid. That I would write another book. How astonishing, and how inevitable.

Karl began to shake, and I wrapped my arms around him and held on as tightly as I could.

ACKNOWLEDGMENTS

I would like to thank my writing teachers, Stuart Dybek, Jaimy Gordon, and John Smolens, for opening my eyes to the particular and for helping me to understand that here lies everything. I would also like to thank my wife, Heather Slomski, for her love, support, and editorial help. And, finally, I would like to thank my family, who have always listened to me; I wouldn't be telling stories today without their patience when I was four.

"Sweet Miseries" first appeared in *Gettysburg Review*.

"Ride the Comet" first appeared in *Alaska Quarterly Review*.

"A Rabbit for Alyosha" first appeared in *Madison Review*.

"The Yellow Scooter" first appeared in *Roanoke Review*.

"Plastic Fantastic" first appeared in the anthology *The Way North*.

"Instead of What We Could Have Said" first appeared in *Contrary Magazine*.

"Floodplain" first appeared in *Big Fiction*.

"The Beginning of Loss" first appeared in *ROPES*.

ABOUT THE AUTHOR

Vincent Reusch's fiction has appeared in a number of national literary journals, including *Gettysburg Review*, *Madison Review*, and *Alaska Quarterly Review*. His work has also been recognized in a number of contests, including the DANA Award Portfolio Contest and the Amazon Breakthrough Novel Award. He lives with his wife and sons in Minnesota, where he teaches and practices the art of writing.

ABOUT
NEW RIVERS PRESS

New Rivers Press emerged from a drafty Massachusetts barn in winter 1968. Intent on publishing work by new and emerging poets, founder C.W. "Bill" Truesdale labored for weeks over an old Chandler & Price letterpress to publish three hundred fifty copies of Margaret Randall's collection *So Many Rooms Has a House but One Roof*. About four hundred titles later, New Rivers is now a nonprofit learning press, based since 2001 at Minnesota State University Moorhead. Charles Baxter, one of the first authors with New Rivers, calls the press "the hidden backbone of the American literary tradition."

As a learning press, New Rivers guides student editors, designers, writers, and filmmakers through the various processes involved in selecting, editing, designing, publishing, and distributing literary books. In working, learning, and interning with New Rivers Press, students gain integral real-world knowledge that they bring with them into the publishing workforce at positions with publishers across the country, or to begin their own small presses and literary magazines.

Please visit our website: newriverspress.com for more information.